THE *Favored* COWBOY

A Shanahan Match
Calling on the Matchmaker
Saved by the Matchmaker
A Wager with the Matchmaker
Marrying the Matchmaker

Bride Ships: New Voyages
Finally His Bride
His Treasured Bride
His Perfect Bride
His Unforgettable Bride

Bride Ships Series
A Reluctant Bride
The Runaway Bride
A Bride of Convenience
Almost a Bride

Orphan Train Series
An Awakened Heart: A Novella
With You Always
Together Forever
Searching for You

Beacons of Hope Series
Out of the Storm: A Novella
Love Unexpected
Hearts Made Whole
Undaunted Hope
Forever Safe
Never Forget

Hearts of Faith Collection
The Preacher's Bride
The Doctor's Lady
Rebellious Heart

Michigan Brides Collection
Unending Devotion
A Noble Groom
Captured by Love

Historical
Luther and Katharina
Newton & Polly

Knights of Brethren Series
Enamored
Entwined
Ensnared
Enriched
Enflamed
Entrusted

Fairest Maidens Series
Beholden
Beguiled
Besotted

Lost Princesses Series

Always: Prequel Novella

Evermore

Foremost

Hereafter

Noble Knights Series

The Vow: Prequel Novella

An Uncertain Choice

A Daring Sacrifice

For Love & Honor

A Loyal Heart

A Worthy Rebel

Waters of Time Series

Come Back to Me

Never Leave Me

Stay With Me

Wait for Me

THE *Favored* COWBOY

JODY HEDLUND

NORTHERN LIGHTS PRESS

The Favored Cowboy
Northern Lights Press
© 2025 by Jody Hedlund
Jody Hedlund Print Edition
ISBN 979-8-9896277-8-3

Jody Hedlund www.jodyhedlund.com

This is a work of historical reconstruction; the appearances of certain historical figures are accordingly inevitable. All other characters are products of the author's imagination. Any resemblance to actual events or locales or persons, living or dead, is entirely coincidental.

Cover Design by roseannawhitedesigns.com
Cover images from Shutterstock

A mail-order bride in Colorado. That's what her life had been reduced to.

Amelia Stone shuddered and drew her thin coat tighter. The mid-December high-country air was drier and more brittle than in New York. But it wasn't the cold that was haunting her so much as what was waiting for her at the end of her journey—marriage to a stranger.

"Almost there," said the man on the horse ahead of hers, his little boy of three riding on the saddle in front of him. The man's wife led their small caravan, carrying her newborn in a sling beneath her fur blanket.

Amelia nodded wearily and laid a hand over her abdomen and the babe growing inside her. If she wore her clothes loosely, the swell didn't show much, but the baby would soon be too big to hide if her calculations were correct. Thankfully, so far she hadn't felt too tired or sick, with only a little indigestion once in a while.

"You can see Breckenridge, Miss Stone." The man spoke again. "There." He pointed ahead to a bend in the Blue River—the river they'd been following since descending Independence Pass.

In the growing dusk, the outline of a town was visible against the backdrop of the towering Tenmile Range. A hodgepodge of weathered log structures as well as whitewashed clapboard buildings clustered along the river and among stumps. Lights shone from windows, and smoke curled from chimneys, giving Breckenridge a welcoming aura. At least, she hoped it would be more welcoming than Albany had been.

It was certainly more picturesque. In fact, from the first moment she'd seen the Rockies from the train window on the plains, she hadn't stopped being awed by the rugged grandeur and beauty of the peaks and the vast wilderness that covered the mountainsides.

With the fresh dusting of snow, the small town ahead had a Christmassy charm and was prettier than Fairplay, where she'd been stuck for the past month while the snow and ice prevented travel. Not only had the weather been an issue, but she'd also had a difficult time finding someone to take her over Independence Pass up into Summit County. She might have been stuck in Fairplay all winter if not for Mr. . . .

Amelia scrambled to make her mind work through the haze that had been there for weeks. What was the fellow's name? Was it Olson? No, it had to do with a tree. Oak? Mr. Oak? That didn't sound quite right. The truth was, she'd never been very good at names, and the pregnancy had made it worse.

Fortunately, Mr. Oak—or whatever his name was—had heard she was looking for a guide to take her to Breckenridge. The kindly man had a business there—a sawmill—that he wanted to check on. He also had family in the area and planned to stay with them through Christmas, which was only two weeks away. With the bright sunshine of the past few days having melted some of the snow, he'd decided to make the trip and had loaned her the horse for the journey.

The trek up into the mountains had been slow and had taken most of the day. They'd had to stop on occasion for the baby. Then, in the higher elevations, the snow had been deep and difficult for the horses to wade through.

Finally, the end was in sight.

Would she meet her husband-to-be tonight? A part of her wanted to get the introduction over with. But another part relished the prospect of waiting a little longer.

A gust of wind tugged at the hood of her coat. She reached up to clasp it in place, but it fell back to her shoulders. Strands of her soft brown hair blew across her cheeks and into her eyes. She secured her hood again, then tucked the long hair back inside.

Her hair was one of her best features. Thick, luxurious, and wavy. Most importantly, it was the one thing she'd gotten from her father and not her mother. Unfortunately, she'd inherited everything else from her mother—her hazel eyes with the flecks of gold, rounded face with dimples in her cheeks, lushly full lips, thick sculpted eyebrows. Amelia not only had her mother's facial features but also her womanly figure—a generous bust, curvy hips, and long legs.

The natural beauty had brought Amelia attention over recent years, including Charles's. She hadn't encouraged him during his visits out to their dairy farm, but he'd noticed her anyway.

Amelia sighed and forced her thoughts away from Charles. The two months of being married to him had been unpleasant until he'd been murdered, but she was hopefully entering into a better arrangement. Anything would be better. That's what she'd been telling herself since answering several ads in the matrimonial catalog back in August.

"Have you remembered your husband-to-be's name yet?" Mr. Oak tossed her another glance, his eyes filled with compassion beneath the brim of his cowboy hat.

"Not yet." Amelia searched her mind again for the

name of the man from Breckenridge with whom she'd exchanged letters. Was it Samuel Beckett? Or was that one she'd written to in California or Oregon? Wasn't the fellow she'd communicated with in Breckenridge a Thomas? Timothy? Or some other *T* name?

Of the three men, she'd picked the one in Breckenridge because he worked with cows and cattle and other livestock. More than that, she liked how he'd answered her question about what the most important qualities were to him. He'd said he was honest, hard-working, and loyal. And that he'd earned the respect of his boss and the people in the community.

A respectable husband. That's what she wanted this time. Hopefully that's what she would get in the man from Breckenridge.

The trouble was, at some point in her journey, she'd lost the bundle of letters from the men. She hadn't realized that she didn't have the correspondences anymore until she'd arrived in Fairplay and searched for them to reread the letters from the fellow in Breckenridge and familiarize herself with him again. She hadn't been able to find them anywhere and had no idea where she'd left them during her days of traveling.

She'd decided her only option was to show up in Breckenridge and make inquiries about who might be expecting a mail-order bride. Yes, she'd originally said she would arrive in the spring. But when she'd realized she was pregnant, she'd decided to move up her departure and travel while she still could.

She hoped the Breckenridge fellow would be willing to marry her sooner rather than later. Her funds were almost gone, and she wouldn't have enough to pay for room and board through spring. If he wasn't ready, she was hoping he would be kind enough to help her out as much as he was able.

What was his name? Thornton? That sounded vaguely familiar.

"Do you have a description of him?" Mr. Oak called over his shoulder.

What had the Breckenridge man said about his appearance? She couldn't remember which one of the men had light or dark hair or blue or green eyes. It didn't really matter. In being married to Charles, she'd learned that a fellow's looks were far less important than his character. That's why she'd made sure all three men she'd corresponded with had stellar characters.

"What about his age?" This question came from her guide's wife, whose name Amelia did remember. Serena.

"I believe he's in his twenties." All the men had been. Not that she particularly cared about age any more than she did appearance.

Mr. Oak shook his head. "Reckon that could be true for most of the single men in Breckenridge."

"Yes," Amelia responded, "but how many specifically

work with cows and cattle?"

"A good number. You'd be surprised how many ranches and farms are up here in the high country, especially in the river valley."

Not for the first time, Amelia wanted to slap herself for neglecting to bring the correspondences. At the very least, before leaving the house in Albany, she could have looked at the name of the man from Breckenridge and clarified it. But those last few days and hours had been so tense as she'd laid out her plan of escape, and she'd been more scattered than usual.

She surveyed the town again as it loomed closer. It didn't look overly large. Surely it wouldn't be too hard to find her husband-to-be. "I'm planning to announce that I've arrived and then pray the fellow hears about me and comes to meet me."

"We'll help you." Serena gave her a reassuring smile. "And I'm sure it will all work out just fine."

Mr. Oak shrugged. "Reckon if he don't come claim you, you'll find another fellow to marry in no time."

Amelia's gaze settled on a wide two-story building on the edge of town. Big black letters were painted across the front above the door: *Vance Hotel.* Light filled each window, and the establishment appeared to be busy.

Maybe she could take a room there tonight. At the very least, she could stop and inquire about her groom. Then, yes, if the fellow from Breckenridge didn't come forward, she would have to find someone else. After all, except for the man having godly morals and being well-respected, not a whole lot else mattered.

She pressed a hand against her abdomen again. Whether she found the original man she'd corresponded with or someone else, she would have to say something about the baby, wouldn't she? She couldn't deceive anyone into thinking the baby was his. That was unconscionable. And she was too far along.

However, the same question plagued her now as it had since she'd left Albany. Would the fellow be interested in her if he knew she was pregnant? She hadn't known about her delicate condition when she'd written the letters in response to the marriage catalog advertisements. But she had let them know she was a widow. So the pregnancy might not come as too much of a surprise.

Mr. Oak bent lower to speak with his little son, as he'd done all throughout the trip. It was easy to see he was a good father and loved his family. She could only pray her husband-to-be would be the same.

Serena slowed her mount to ride beside Amelia's. She wore a scarf over her head and another one around her neck, so that only her pretty face showed, revealing her bright eyes and rosy cheeks. "Please come out to the ranch and stay with us, Miss Stone."

"I couldn't impose."

"Weston's family will gladly welcome you."

Weston. Ah, yes. That was her guide's name.

"I was once in a difficult situation too." Serena's eyes held a compassion that reached out and tugged at Amelia's heart. "I know what it's like to be alone in a new town without any support. And with a child . . ."

Serena's gaze slid to Amelia's middle for a brief moment, and it was enough for Amelia to know Serena had guessed she was pregnant.

"Thank you." Amelia hadn't had any support since she'd married Charles and moved off the dairy farm, leaving her father behind. The union had been the only way to save the farm. However, in the end, her efforts hadn't mattered. Her father had died of a heart attack only a month after her marriage.

Weston glanced at Serena, as he had frequently, clearly making sure she and the baby were secure. Then he nodded at Amelia. "Reckon you can stay with my brother and his wife as long as you need."

"That's very kind." Amelia's throat tightened. These two strangers had shown her more consideration in one day than anyone in Albany had shown her in the few months she'd lived there.

"We'll stop at a couple places in town," Weston said, "and put out word about your situation and that you'll be staying at the ranch."

"If you're sure . . ."

"Of course we're sure." Serena smiled warmly.

"That would be wonderful."

Weston tipped up his cowboy hat and surveyed the edge of town. "If the fellow is still living in the area, then he can come out to the ranch, and you can make sure he's decent before going off with him."

That was so thoughtful and considerate. Amelia's throat closed up even more, and she couldn't respond. All she could do was offer him a wobbly smile—one she hoped contained her gratefulness.

Weston smiled in return, then shifted forward in his saddle, his legs straddling his little boy, who was holding the reins.

Within minutes, they were at Vance Hotel. Weston offered to go in and inquire on Amelia's behalf, but Serena suggested they all take a moment to warm up before riding the last of the distance to High Country Ranch, which was apparently a couple miles north of Breckenridge.

As they stepped inside, the front room opened into a spacious dining room filled with a dozen small tables. Most were occupied by men and a few women eating supper—roast with carrots and potatoes along with slices of thick bread and bowls of custard.

Cigar smoke cast a haze over the few oil lanterns hanging from the ceiling. Somehow, Amelia ended up under one of the lanterns, making it seem as though a spotlight shone right on her. All eyes turned their way, landing upon her just as she tossed off her hood and her hair spilled in long waves around her.

A hush came over the dining room, accentuating the clanking of pots and pans through an open door that led to the kitchen.

She was the center of attention, just like when she'd been in Fairplay.

She had the urge to duck back outside and let Weston take care of things for her after all. But he was busy behind her, helping Serena unbundle their children.

Amelia straightened her shoulders. She didn't need his help with this. This was her problem and not his.

She tried to offer the crowd a smile, hoping it didn't look like a grimace. "Hi, everyone. I'm hoping someone will be able to direct me to the man in your community who sent away for a mail-order bride."

"You a mail-order bride?" asked an older gentleman at the closest table. With dusty clothing and a soot-covered face, his shoulders were slumped and his features drooping. He sat with two other men who were equally dusty and tired, although their eyes regarded her with curiosity.

"Yes, I've lost my correspondence and cannot recall the fellow's name, but he should have letters from me. I wrote to him a couple of times."

The room was silent for a moment.

"I'm from the East . . . New York—"

"If she's from New York"—another male voice came from a side table, this one from a young man with blond hair, his eyes alight with interest—"then she's gotta be the one Thatcher's been waiting for."

A *T* name. But Thatcher? "Thatcher." She spoke the name, hoping it would jog her memory.

"Yep, Thatcher Hoyt."

Hoyt? That name couldn't be right. It didn't sound familiar, and surely she would recognize it if it belonged to one of the men she'd corresponded with. "He works with livestock—mostly cattle and horses."

"Then that's him," said the same young man. "The veterinarian."

"Gotta be Thatcher," said another voice from among the many. "He's been riding into town practically every day, keeping a lookout for his bride."

Why had he been riding to town every day when she'd told him she was coming in the spring? That didn't make sense.

"He reckoned his bride wouldn't come 'til spring." This came from the older man at the nearby table, as though he'd heard her silent question. "But he was still hoping you'd make it before winter."

Had she given her groom some indication she would come earlier? Maybe in her last letter, he'd sensed the fears and frustration that had plagued her after Charles's murder, even though she hadn't disclosed any details except that she was a widow.

"Mr. Hoyt's gonna be plumb tickled!"

"He didn't tell us she was such a looker."

"He's one lucky fellow."

"She's a real beauty."

The clamor in the dining room rose.

They all seemed convinced that this Thatcher Hoyt was her groom.

He hadn't mentioned anything about being a veterinarian that she remembered from the letters. But the correspondences had been brief, hardly more than a couple of paragraphs each. The men couldn't be expected to communicate everything about themselves in such a short time. She sure hadn't.

"Is this fellow the only one in town expecting a bride?" she called out above the hubbub. "Are there any others?"

The voices quieted.

Behind her, Serena's baby gave a tiny wail, probably of hunger. Weston was speaking to a gentleman who seemed to be the proprietor.

"I know of a fellow who works at Little Boy Mine." A stocky man sitting near the hearth spoke first. "He sent away for a bride, but she's coming from Boston."

"Ain't the Noble Ranch foreman sending away for a bride too?" asked another.

"Yep," said the young man with the blond hair. "But I heard Beckett got engaged to one of those Berkley women. The younger sister."

Beckett? That sounded familiar. And a ranch foreman would certainly work with livestock. But if he was marrying someone else, then she wouldn't be able to count on him to take her in.

Thatcher, the veterinarian, had to be the one. Besides, if he was eagerly awaiting her arrival, that had to be a good sign.

She swept her gaze over the faces peering back at her. "Is Thatcher well-respected in this community?"

"He's a real nice fellow," called someone.

"A mite young to be a veterinarian," said the old-timer sitting closest to her. "Not as experienced as we need in these parts."

"But he goes out on calls whenever anyone needs him," the younger fellow countered.

A man near the back of the room stood. "He came out in a thunderstorm and saved my sow when she had trouble during her birthing."

"He's as honest and kind as they come," said another. "Let's get him on in here, and you can see for yourself."

The young man with blond hair stood from his chair and started for the door. "I'll go fetch him."

Another fellow stood. "I'll go after the reverend since it looks like we're gonna have a wedding tonight."

A wedding tonight?

Amelia took a tiny step back. She hadn't been sure if she'd meet the fellow tonight, much less marry him.

Weston was standing in the doorway of the side room, his back turned on the dining room. No doubt he'd found a warm place for Serena to nurse the baby and wasn't paying attention to the drama unfolding.

Amelia swallowed, pushing down her misgivings. If this fellow—this veterinarian—was her groom, then what was the point of waiting for a wedding? She'd only inconvenience Serena and Weston and their family, and she'd only be putting off the inevitable. After all, she'd come west to get married. Ready or not, that's what she planned to do.

At the clomping of horse hooves coming down the lane toward his house, Thatcher Hoyt stepped out of the barn and held up the lantern so that his visitor would know where to find him. Rusty was already barking a welcome and hobbling off to greet the newcomer.

If Thatcher had to guess who was coming, he'd pick Mr. Mintz, the middle-aged farmer who ran a grist mill outside of Breckenridge.

Earlier in the day, Mr. Mintz had stopped Thatcher on his way past his farm and asked him to take a look at a lame mare. One glance at the blood from the coffin bone protruding through the sole had been all Thatcher needed to know. The horse had foundered. The disease of the hooves was a hard one to cure and painful for the horse.

Mr. Mintz had wanted a quick cure, but Thatcher had explained that the only way the horse could be saved from founder was by a lot of time and attention—

cleaning the wound, changing the dressing multiple times a day, keeping the stall spotless, and giving the horse feed that wasn't so rich.

Not many farmers were willing to devote such attention to a lame horse, not with how many other demands they had, and Mr. Mintz had been no exception. He'd claimed the bandage Thatcher wrapped around the hoof would be enough. As Thatcher had readied to leave, he'd instructed Mr. Mintz to send word if the horse's condition got any worse and he decided to put the horse down. Thatcher had told Mr. Mintz he'd be willing to take the horse from him if there was a small chance of saving her.

He raised the lantern higher. The beams cut through the darkness of the evening, revealing the log-cabin home that had come with the place he was renting. It was small and weathered, but the construction was sound and the chinking solid. The roof was also in good condition, made of hand-split shingles.

The area around the house and barn had been cleared of trees and most stumps for farming. A large field close to the house contained strawberries and rhubarb. Farther out, the land had been cultivated into hay.

Thatcher had been too busy to keep up with the fruit last summer, and the birds had eaten most of it, but he'd managed to harvest the hay. The solicitor of the property, Maverick Oakley, who was related to the owner, had allowed Thatcher to sell the hay and keep the profits. Thatcher had used it to stock up on more medicine and supplies before winter prevented wagon trains from bringing up goods from Denver.

The horse and rider had slowed beside the cabin but then must have seen the lantern, because in the next instant they were continuing down the lane that curved around to the barn.

"Thatcher?" came a man's voice that was decidedly younger than Mr. Mintz's.

Thatcher waved an arm. "Over here by the barn!"

If this wasn't Mr. Mintz, who was it?

As the horse drew nearer, the lantern light fell across a young man wearing a battered Stetson, his blond hair showing underneath. It was Jeremy Usher, the blacksmith's assistant. Even though he was four or five years younger than Thatcher's twenty-five years, Jeremy was a fun-loving fellow, and Thatcher had enjoyed his company on occasion, along with some of the other single men who worked in town.

Although Thatcher had blond hair too, his was a shade lighter because he spent more time out in the sunshine than Jeremy. Thatcher was also stockier, with broader shoulders and thicker arms and legs from his days as a farmer boy, plowing fields, wrangling cows, and harvesting crops.

What was Jeremy doing out tonight? Coming to

invite him to another dance at Inman's Lodge or to watch a hockey game on the manmade ice-skating pond on the edge of town?

Thatcher was more than ready for some company or excitement. It didn't matter how tired he was or that he'd had many sleepless nights lately thanks to all the vaccinations he'd been doing for blackleg. The deadly disease had killed off close to twenty of the Nobles' cattle before Sterling had called on him and given him the go-ahead to administer the vaccine. Over the past two weeks since then, Thatcher had been called to two other ranches, and so far, the vaccine seemed to be putting an end to the spread of the disease.

Thatcher had studied that particular vaccine and worked on developing it during his years at the Veterinary College of Philadelphia. He believed in it and its ability. But he also knew that anything could go wrong in the blink of an eye.

He'd learned that the hard way earlier in the year when he'd made a mistake that had cost him his practice near Cedar Rapids. Not only had it cost him his livelihood, but he'd lost everything—his reputation, respect, honor, trustworthiness, and even his fiancée.

He'd had no choice but to move from Iowa to someplace far away where no one had heard about his blunder. With his cousin Lee living in Summit County and writing back home to family about the beauty of the wilderness and mountains, Thatcher had packed the little he'd had left and come just as soon as the snow had melted on the high mountain passes.

Breckenridge, in the high country of Colorado, had seemed like the ends of the earth back in May when he'd arrived. But after the summer and autumn of settling in—especially after moving out of his cousin's house and to the farm—he'd realized the area was a slice of heaven on earth.

Except for the loneliness . . .

He hated being alone and always had. He enjoyed being around people, having company, and carrying on conversations. That meant he relished making calls at any time of the day or night.

But his calls weren't enough. He still had far too much time alone. In fact, five minutes alone was too much and one of the downsides of being so sociable and outgoing.

"Howdy, Thatcher." Jeremy wore a wide grin as he reined in, and his eyes held excitement.

"Good to see you, Jeremy." Thatcher reached for the bridle and rubbed a hand over the horse's muzzle.

"Go put on your Sunday suit." Jeremy thumbed the air in the direction of the cabin. "You're getting married tonight."

"Married?" Thatcher's hand stalled on the horse's forehead, and the word rolled through Thatcher's head in a strange vacuum. But in the next instant, understanding hit him. He couldn't hold back a wide grin of his own. "My bride finally arrived?"

"Yep. She just rode into town with Weston Oakley and his family."

"Thank the good Lord." A thrill raced through Thatcher's blood. "Finally."

"Knew you'd be happy." Jeremy began to dismount.

Happy didn't even begin to describe how Thatcher was feeling. It was more like elated, even relieved. He'd started communicating with Eileen back in July, shortly after he'd moved to the farm and realized how big and lonely the place was all by himself, and after he'd realized how few single women lived in the area.

Eileen was from New York City and had been working as a domestic for a couple of years. She was ready to leave the city behind, and after hearing about the West and the mountains, she'd responded to his advertisement about moving to his farm up in the mountains. She'd said she would do her best to arrive in the autumn. After her last letter in September, he'd expected her to arrive by October, early November at the latest.

With the long winter looming ahead, he hadn't wanted to be alone, had even considered returning to town and living with Lee, his wife Dot, and their three young children again.

The trouble with moving was that he needed space for

all his equipment, medicine, and the horse he'd purchased after he'd rented the farm. He'd also, as usual, acquired a menagerie of pets that he'd rescued or been given by people who no longer wanted them—two sheep, three goats, a duck, and a handful of chickens.

Then there was Rusty, a dark-red golden retriever who was missing one of her back legs.

The dog limped next to Thatcher.

Jeremy's feet had barely touched the ground before Rusty was lifting her friendly face, thumping her tail back and forth, and begging for attention.

"Did she say what took her so long?" Thatcher took up the lead line of Jeremy's horse and wrapped it around the corral fence post.

"Didn't have time to inquire." Jeremy scratched Rusty's head. "And you don't have time to waste with questions. Go get ready." Jeremy gave Thatcher a shove toward the cabin. "I'll saddle your horse."

Thatcher stumbled but caught himself, walking backward for several paces. He supposed it didn't really matter what had held Eileen up. She was here now, and that was all that mattered. "Does she seem nice?"

"Real nice." Jeremy's grin was so wide it rivaled the Great Plains. "And she's a real beauty."

"Really?"

"Yep," Jeremy said. "She's prettier than any gal I've ever seen."

"Then she must be modest, because in her letters she claimed her features were plain."

"Nothin' plain about your woman."

Thatcher's blood began to hum with a new anticipation. He'd been prepared for plain, had been content with that. But now that she was here and was pretty—at least according to Jeremy—he wouldn't mind. Not in the least. Most importantly, Eileen was kind and caring—at least, that's how she'd seemed from her letters.

"Reckon if you decide you don't want her, I'll be first in line to marry her."

"Oh, I'll want her." Thatcher turned and began to jog toward the cabin. "You better believe I'll want her."

He'd been eager to get married to Nora too. After they'd called off their engagement, he'd been hurt and disappointed, but there had been so much else going on that he hadn't really missed her. Or maybe he'd never really loved her enough to fight to keep her.

Whatever the case, after months of being alone, he'd had the time to get over her and move on. Now no one and nothing was stopping him from getting married tonight. That was for sure.

Thatcher was ready to leave for town in record time. He could hardly contain his anticipation and found his nerves increasing the closer he got to Breckenridge. He was grateful for Jeremy's companionship and questions about how the marriage ads worked. The discussion kept

Thatcher distracted and from being too nervous.

The ad hadn't been all that hard to place in the *Matrimonial News*, which was sold on street corners by newsboys right alongside other newspapers. The advertisements cost twenty-five cents and had to convey height, weight, and personal appearance as well as financial and social position in life using only forty words or less.

To avoid publishing names and addresses, the advertisements were numbered. When finding an ad that looked like a potential match, the person replied to the *Matrimonial News* office. From there, the inquiry was passed along to the appropriate person.

Eileen had responded to his advertisement, and then they'd exchanged several letters before he'd asked her to come to Breckenridge and be his wife. The last correspondence had been her letter of affirmation.

He could admit he'd been somewhat skeptical of the process when he'd first looked into doing it. But it had worked out well for several men in Summit County that he'd gotten to know, and he'd decided it was likely the best—and perhaps only—way of finding a wife in the West, where there was a shortage of marriageable women.

Eileen had seemed like a genuinely nice person from her letters. She'd claimed to love family and wanted a large one of her own. She'd said she loved animals, that she'd grown up with a few livestock. And she was proficient in taking care of a home because her work as a domestic had prepared her well for being a wife.

They hadn't exchanged pictures. He hadn't brought any photographs of himself along in his move to Colorado, and she'd claimed she'd never had her picture taken. But she'd described herself as having brown hair and eyes, being average in height and weight, and having features that were plain.

Obviously a person's appearance was subjective. What might be plain to somebody could very well be beautiful to someone else. However, if she was truly as beautiful as Jeremy described, then she had to know she wasn't *plain*.

Did that mean she'd lied about her looks? If she hadn't been honest about her appearance, were there other things she might have exaggerated?

The thought unsettled Thatcher. He'd known the risk involved in putting an advertisement out there for a wife. He'd heard the stories of false descriptions that made people sound better than they really were. He'd even heard stories about people using the advertisements as a way to scam others out of money.

Of course, Eileen wouldn't be able to scam him for money since he didn't have much. He never had the heart to require payments, even though he had fees for his services. If someone was having a hard time, he always told them to pay him whenever they could. Others paid him in whatever means they had—food or grain or a chicken.

Thatcher never minded, though. He hadn't become a veterinarian to make money. He'd done it because he loved animals.

As he and Jeremy started through town, several fellows on the street congratulated him on his upcoming nuptials. Thatcher wasn't surprised at how many people already knew about his bride's arrival and the wedding. Most people knew he'd been waiting for her, mainly because he was so eager and had talked about it with anyone who would listen.

Yes, he had a big mouth. He talked about everything. But for good or bad, that's just the way he was.

When they reached the opposite side of town and neared Vance Hotel, a crowd was milling around outside. At the sight of him, people began to cheer and clap and whistle.

As he dismounted, men slapped his back and congratulated him. Through it all, his grin only got bigger, and his heart swelled with affection for this community that had welcomed him in as one of their own.

"She's waiting inside for you," said Mr. Vance, the owner of the inn, as he held the door open. A short man with a rotund stomach, he was known for his good cooking. "Gave her a table and a warm meal to tide her over until you got here."

"I'm obliged." Thatcher followed him through the

doorway and swiped off his hat.

The dining room was just as congested as the outside, with people standing around and all the tables and chairs full. He searched for a woman who met Eileen's description and landed upon a table at the center, where Weston Oakley and his wife Serena were sitting with their little tyke and baby. Eileen was positioned so that he couldn't really see her, just her back and some long strands of hair hanging loose while others were fashionably coiled. She had slender shoulders and a graceful poise.

Seeing just this part of her was enough for him to realize that Jeremy was right. Eileen was a real beauty. He didn't have to see her face to know that.

The room began to quiet, and all attention swung to where he stood, just inside the door next to Mr. Vance. Others were crowding behind him, threatening to push him forward.

As silence settled, Eileen placed her fork upon her plate, picked up her napkin and blotted her mouth, then stiffened her shoulders, as though bracing herself to turn around and meet him. What would she think? Would he meet her expectations?

He combed his fingers through his loose hair, hoping to rid himself of a hat ring and appear presentable.

Eileen seemed to be exchanging silent communication with Weston and Serena. Thatcher didn't know them well, since they lived in Fairplay. But he had seen them one other time when they'd made the journey up to the High Country Ranch to visit with family.

With a nod from Serena, Eileen pushed back from the table, then slowly rose to her feet. She had on a simple long blue calico skirt paired with a white blouse. She hesitated a moment, then pivoted.

He drew in a sharp breath. From her light brown hair to the tips of her boots, she was dream-worthy. Her face was round with the hint of dimples in her cheeks even though she wasn't smiling. She had generous lips and wide eyes that had more green and gold to them than the brown she'd described, or maybe they only appeared to shift colors due to the lighting.

Whatever the case, neither her letters nor Jeremy's description had prepared Thatcher for how stunning she was, and all he could do was stare at her like an idiot.

She was taking him in too, scanning him from his hatless head, all the way down his dark-blue suit to his shiny black dress shoes. As she finished, she lifted her gaze back to his face, and her eyes connected with his.

What did she think of him? Was he what she'd pictured and expected? If so, that made one of them.

Her eyes didn't reveal anything, and neither did her expression. If she was disappointed or relieved, he couldn't tell.

Whatever the case, he had to say something to break

the awkward silence that had settled over the room. "Welcome to Breckenridge."

"Thank you." Her voice didn't contain any hesitation. "After the snow delayed me in Fairplay, I wasn't sure I'd make it."

"You've been in Fairplay?"

"I was told the passes out of Denver were too dangerous with the ice and snow, but that the Ute Pass out of Colorado Springs was still open."

If she'd come in from the southerly direction, then it made sense that she'd ended up stranded in Fairplay.

"I'd still be in Fairplay if not for Weston and Serena." She offered the couple a grateful smile.

The smile brought out her dimples even more. But even with the smile, her expression contained a reservation and seriousness that told him her life hadn't been easy and that she didn't smile often.

"Well, I'm glad you made it."

"*Glad* is an understatement," called a man on the far side of the room. "He's ecstatic."

Chuckles broke out, and someone from behind slapped his back. Of course everyone would tease him about his eagerness for his bride and embarrass him to no end. But he deserved it.

He chuckled himself as he traded a nudge of elbows with Jeremy, who was standing beside him.

"Let's get this wedding started," shouted someone else from outside. Several more men echoed the call.

Thatcher grinned. "Nothing like getting right to the point."

An older man sitting at a nearby table chortled. "You better marry her before someone steals her away from you."

Would that really happen? Thatcher didn't think anyone else in the community would make a claim on Eileen. But maybe it was for the best to marry her tonight, before some other fellow tried to charm her or she had the chance to change her mind.

"The reverend's already here." Mr. Vance nodded to Reverend Livingston, in the clerical collar and black suit, who was standing near the hearth, his prayer book in hand.

The diminutive man was speaking quietly with an older fellow and abruptly ended his conversation. "Are we ready to begin?"

"Sure, why not—" Thatcher stopped short at the sight of Eileen's trembling hand at the neckline of her blouse.

Catching his look, she quickly tucked her hands behind her back, out of sight. She was obviously feeling some trepidation.

He took a step toward her, then stopped. "If you're not ready, we can wait."

She hesitated.

"Really," he insisted. "I don't want to rush you."

Was she ready to get married?

Amelia's heart was quavering almost as much as her hands. This was a life-changing decision. And what if she got herself into another horrible situation like she had with Charles?

No, this was different. Thatcher was different.

A dozen feet away, separated from her by a couple of tables, he stood solidly, his kind eyes upon her. That was one of the first things she'd noticed about him, that he had kind eyes. And he had laugh lines at the corners of his eyes.

Of course, she'd also noted that he was good-looking—but in a muscular country-boy way and not in the suave city-guy way that had befitted Charles.

Besides, every person in the room had testified to Thatcher's good character while she'd eaten dinner and waited for his arrival. With so many in the community speaking highly of him as the veterinarian, it had to be another sign that marrying him was the right decision.

"We don't have to do this tonight," Thatcher said gently and held out a hand, as if he was speaking with a spooked animal.

Maybe she was a little spooked. Weston and Serena had told her again over supper that she was welcome to stay at High Country Ranch with them until she was ready for marriage.

But if Thatcher was a man of good standing and so well-liked by everyone, then what was the point in putting off the wedding for another day or two? Why make things more complicated for Weston and Serena? Why inconvenience the townspeople, the reverend, and even Thatcher? Why not just move forward and do what she'd come for?

Getting married here and now would certainly make things easier for her and everyone.

The only trouble was that she wanted him to know about her pregnancy first. He deserved the opportunity to change his mind if he wasn't willing to raise another man's child as his own. Should she ask for a moment of privacy so she could speak to him about it?

She glanced around the crowded room. Eager and excited faces peered back at her. More eager and excited faces peeked in from the doorway behind Thatcher and the hotel owner. She wasn't sure how big the town was, but it seemed as though half of it was here.

"That settles it." Thatcher's voice rang with decisiveness. "I'm putting off the wedding for a couple of days so we can have the chance to get to know each other first."

Thatcher's gaze reached across the distance and seemed to ask her if his decision made her happy.

A strange lump rose into her throat. When had any man ever cared if she was happy? Of course, her father had loved her dearly and tried to make up for Mother's leaving. But he'd always been so busy and tired. His daughter's happiness hadn't necessarily been his top priority.

"Let's call it a night," Thatcher called out good-naturedly.

Sighs and murmurs of disappointment filtered around her.

"No." She spoke the one word loud enough that hopefully all the people inside and out could hear her. "Everyone is here, and everything is ready. We should have the wedding tonight."

"I agree," came a call across the room.

"No sense in delaying the inevitable," said another.

Thatcher's mouth stalled around a response.

"I came here to marry you," she said, trying to keep her voice steady, "and that's what I intend to do."

At her words, a cheer rose up. With lots of back-thumping and grinning and congratulations, the crowd maneuvered Thatcher toward her. As he reached her side, he raised his brow in question, probably trying to gauge if she meant what she'd said and really wanted to go through with the wedding.

She gave a firm nod and opened her mouth to ask him for a moment alone first, but before she could say anything, the eager crowd was guiding them toward the reverend, in front of the blazing hearth fire.

With more pats and slaps, the men positioned them, then stepped away. But by this point, even more people had pushed into the dining room from outside, so it was more congested than before.

Even if she wanted to cancel—which she didn't—she wouldn't be able to make her way out through the tight crowd.

She stood close enough to Thatcher that her arm nearly brushed against his. Should she have a whispered conversation here and now? Maybe she ought to lean in and just tell him she was pregnant.

He'd straightened to his full height and now towered over her by about six inches. No, she wouldn't be able to reach his ear easily, and she didn't want to risk others hearing her news about the baby. Not until she had the chance to find out how Thatcher felt about it.

She hesitated. What should she do?

Reverend Livingston, whom she'd met a short while

ago, opened his prayer book to a dog-eared page that appeared to be well used. He cleared his throat. "Dearly beloved friends, we are gathered together here in the sight of God and in the face of his congregation, to join together this man and this woman in holy matrimony, which is an honorable estate, instituted by God in Paradise."

The room grew silent, allowing the crackling of the burning wood to be heard.

Now was most definitely not the time to talk to Thatcher about her pregnancy. She would have to wait until later, when they were alone, and tell him then. If he was as kind as he first appeared, surely he would accept her baby from her first marriage. It wouldn't have to change their circumstances.

But obviously, if he was opposed, she would allow him a way out of the marriage, wouldn't hold him to their agreement, and would give him an annulment.

". . . considering the causes for which matrimony was ordained," the reverend was saying as he read from his book. "One was the procreation of children, to be brought up in the fear and nurture of the Lord. Secondly, it was ordained for a remedy against sin and to avoid fornication . . ."

Amelia tried to block out the reverend's words. She didn't want to hear about the references to the marriage bed. The nightly visits from Charles had been uncomfortable and awkward, and she wasn't looking forward to having to endure marital relations again with a new husband. But she also knew it was the price she had to pay for a home and security. Without a husband, she had nothing and no one. She would never be able to survive, especially to take care of the baby.

"Therefore," the reverend continued, "if any man can show any just cause why they may not lawfully be joined together, let him now speak or else hereafter forever hold his peace."

She tensed. What if Thatcher wasn't the right groom? What if there was someone else who was waiting for her?

Surely in a small community like this, that man would come forward now and say something, wouldn't he?

Again, silence stretched through the room, this time broken by coughing.

"Very well," the reverend said. "Then let's proceed with the vows."

Thatcher expelled a breath.

Had he been nervous that another man would step in and prevent their wedding?

Everyone had claimed he was excited about his bride coming and eager to get married. It would appear so. That was another good sign—at least she hoped so.

"You first, Thatcher. Repeat after me." The reverend smoothed the page in front of him. "I, Thatcher, take thee . . ."

"Eileen." Thatcher nodded. "I, Thatcher, take thee, Eileen, to be my wedded wife."

Amelia startled. Who was Eileen? Certainly, Thatcher had just misspoken and meant Amelia. Or what if he'd forgotten her name the same way she had his? Or what if her letter had gotten wet and the name had been blurred? She supposed Amelia and Eileen had some similarities.

"To have and to hold from this day forward," Thatcher continued, "for better, for worse, for richer, for poorer, in sickness and in health, to love and to cherish, till death us do part . . ."

Amelia felt suddenly frozen in place. Should she correct him? Clear up the confusion?

She had to. Would the marriage even be legal if he said the wrong name? She supposed it would. After all, she was there and giving her consent.

"Your turn." Reverend Livingston shifted slightly so that he was angled in her direction. "Repeat after me. I, Eileen, take thee, Thatcher, to be my wedded husband."

Oh my. There was that wrong name again. She couldn't actually refer to herself as Eileen. That would be really odd and wrong. But she also couldn't give her real name of Amelia at this point and have everyone question what was going on. She was surprised Serena and Weston weren't saying something. Of course, they'd called her Miss Stone, which was her maiden name and how she'd introduced herself to them. But she was pretty sure she'd also told them her first name was Amelia.

The whole room seemed to be holding its breath, waiting for her to speak her vows.

The unease she'd been feeling from not saying anything about the pregnancy began to rise inside and clamp around her chest, tightening her breathing. She had to say something.

"I . . . I . . . take thee, Thatcher, to be my wedded husband." There, she'd skipped over the wrong name. That would have to be okay for now. Later, she would have a lot of explaining to do with Thatcher. She just hoped he would be understanding.

The rest of the wedding passed with only one more use of the wrong name. Thatcher gave her a gold wedding band. It was plain but practical, one he'd obviously had ready for the occasion when she arrived.

By the time the reverend stated the benediction, she felt as if she'd just stayed up all night for a calf birthing, except at least with calf birthings, she walked away feeling content.

She felt anything but content as Reverend Livingston finished. "I pronounce that they be man and wife together. In the name of the Father, of the Son, and of the Holy Ghost. Amen."

"Amen," Thatcher murmured with his head bowed and eyes closed. He had taken every part of the ceremony seriously and had been earnest in his declarations and intentions. She was the one who was harboring falsehoods, and she needed to get him alone just as soon as possible and confess everything.

What had happened, though? Was she the woman he'd been waiting for? Or was she another man's bride?

As the reverend closed his book, calls rose up from some of the younger men. "Kiss her!"

Thatcher laughed off their calls. "Later, my friends."

"No, kiss her now!"

Thatcher shifted to face her, his grin in place. "It seems we won't get away without kissing. If you don't mind . . ."

"It's fine, Thatcher." She'd never been fond of Charles's kisses, which thankfully hadn't been frequent. But again, she knew it was part of the physical aspect of being married that she couldn't avoid.

She raised her face so he would have easy access for the kiss.

He dropped his gaze to her mouth and then lifted a hand gently to her cheek. His fingers skimmed the line of her jaw, and then he bent in, his gaze riveted to her mouth.

She closed her eyes and steeled herself for the unpleasantness.

In the next instant, his lips touched hers softly. In fact, the tenderness was so unexpected that she couldn't even begin to compare his kiss to the demanding and hard kisses Charles had always given her.

His lips meshed with hers for only a few seconds, hardly any contact at all, before he pulled back to whistles and cheers.

Thatcher's grin made a quick and charming appearance. It looked good on him.

She released a tense breath, only to have his gaze dart back to her and his grin falter.

"You all right?" he whispered.

He was asking her if she was all right? She couldn't immediately answer. Here was a stranger who had not only been concerned about her happiness moments ago, but was now asking her if she was all right?

She nodded.

"You sure?" he whispered again.

"Yes, I'm not used to anyone asking that."

His brow rose, as though her statement had taken him aback.

She had to offer him a smile, and somehow forced her lips to curve upward.

"Might as well get used to it." He reached for her hand and tucked it into the crook of his arm. "Because I'll be asking it a lot."

At the sincerity in his words and in his eyes, she could feel the stiffness melting away from her smile and it turning genuine.

She liked Thatcher. What was his last name—the

name that she'd now taken as hers?

She searched for it only a moment before putting aside the effort, knowing she would hear it again soon enough from one of the townspeople.

"Are you ready to go home?" he asked.

Home. She hadn't called any place home other than the dairy farm she'd grown up on. Like many of the other dairy farms in the countryside outside of Albany, they'd had a small herd of only two dozen cows. But it had kept her father and her busy morning and night all year round.

The drought a couple of years ago had been the start of their financial problems, just as it had been for many other farmers. Those who hadn't relied solely on dairy for the income had been able to survive better. But her father and others like him, who had made a living off selling milk, had been forced to take out loans to survive. Except with loan sharks like Charles, survival wasn't really possible. Not when the fees for the loans and the interest rates made the loans too high to pay back.

Whatever the case, Amelia hadn't considered the house in Albany with Charles home. She wasn't sure if she'd ever feel at home here in Breckenridge either. But she had to make an effort, especially for her baby. She wanted to wipe the slate clean here where no one had to know about Charles and all of his crimes.

Could she start over with Thatcher? So far, in the short time she'd known him, he'd proven himself to be more well-liked, friendly, polite, and considerate than Charles had ever been.

Thatcher was obviously a catch worth keeping, and now that she had him, she didn't want to do anything to jeopardize things.

Did that mean she should keep silent about her real name? And the baby? Maybe at least until Thatcher had the chance to get to know her and learn to like her? In a week or two she could confess everything, and maybe by then, he wouldn't want an annulment.

But wasn't honesty one of the top characteristics she'd wanted in her new husband? How could she require honesty from him if she wasn't willing to be truthful in return?

No, the best thing was for her to tell Thatcher the truth about herself. She would just need to find the right moment to do so and hope that he would still want her.

"I'll return the horse tomorrow," Thatcher called to Weston as the fellow, his wife, and their little ones continued down the road toward High Country Ranch.

"No hurry!" Weston's response echoed in the cold night.

Thatcher gave the family a final wave, then raised his lantern higher to illuminate the lane that led to his cabin and barn.

The light fell across Eileen, on the horse beside him with two large carpet bags strapped to the back of her mount. She hadn't brought much with her. He'd expected a couple of trunks at least. But maybe as a maid, she'd never accumulated much.

She'd been quiet for most of the ride out of town and seemed content to let him do most of the talking with Weston and Serena. He hadn't minded, although a part of him had selfishly wanted to ride home with just his new wife so he could spend the time getting to know her.

Eileen watched Weston and Serena ride away, as if she wasn't quite ready for them to leave. Was she nervous about spending time alone with him? Their meeting had been abrupt and their wedding rushed, giving them little time to converse.

Yet, they had all winter to talk and become comfortable with one another. The awkwardness wouldn't last long. At least, he'd do his best to put her at ease.

Probably the first thing he should do to alleviate her worries was talk about the marital expectations. Of course he wanted a real marriage with all the benefits. But he also wanted a marriage with affection and companionship, which would be harder to develop since they were starting out with nothing.

He'd had plenty of time to think about things over the past weeks while waiting for her to arrive, and he'd decided it would be best if they had a period to get to know each other before . . . well, before having all those marriage benefits.

If he told her his decision, would that help her to relax around him? After all, he didn't want her to think he was taking her to his cabin and going straight to the bedroom. He couldn't imagine doing something so cold and impersonal. No, when he joined her in the bedroom, he wanted her to welcome him not just out of duty but because she wanted him there with her.

"So, this is my—our home." He shifted the lantern again so that the lane lined with trees was more distinguishable, since the sliver of the moon wasn't providing much light. "I'm renting the place. But once I get enough saved, I'm hoping to buy a small farm of my own."

"That sounds nice."

He wasn't sure when he'd ever have enough saved, but that was his goal. "In the meantime, I hope you'll like living here."

"I'm sure I will." She seemed to be taking in the property as best she could in the darkness.

Rusty's barking from near the cabin told him the golden retriever had noticed them and was welcoming them home. "That's my dog, Rusty."

"Thatcher?" Her voice held a note of hesitation . . . and something else that set him suddenly on edge.

"Yes?"

"I need to tell you two things."

"Okay." He had the feeling he wasn't going to like either of the things. But what could he do about it now that he was married to her? All he'd be able to do was make the best of it. At least, he hoped he could do that. "Would you like to go into the cabin first and get out of the cold?"

"My name isn't Eileen. It's Amelia." Her words came

out in a rush.

What? Amelia? Where had that come from? The three letters she'd written to him had all been signed with Eileen.

He opened his mouth to respond, but the declaration had left him speechless, which didn't happen often.

"The other thing you should know about me . . ." She drew in a breath, one that shuddered, as though she dreaded what she had to say next.

That dread penetrated him, sending a cold trail up his spine.

"The thing is . . ." The lantern highlighted the lighter brown strands in her hair and the curves of her face, along with her dimples. Even as serious as she was at the moment, nothing could hide those puckers. What would it be like to kiss them?

Inwardly he gave himself a shake. He couldn't think about that now.

"I mentioned I was a widow, but . . ."

She was a widow? "No, you didn't tell me."

"I didn't?" Her eyes widened. "I thought I did to each of the men I was writing to."

"You were writing to more men than me?" That was news too. He'd thought he was the only one. At least, that's how it had sounded.

"I corresponded with three."

"I didn't realize that."

"Yes, I wanted to find a man of good character and thought by having more than one option, that would help."

"So I had the best character?"

She gave a slight shrug of her shoulders. "I favored you above the other two because of how well-respected you are. I also appreciated that we both like animals and livestock."

At least he'd gotten that right about her.

"So your real name is Amelia? And you've been married already?"

"Yes to both." She tugged her coat about her more securely, a puff of her breath showing in the air.

"We should get inside and warm up—"

"I'm pregnant."

That was obviously the second thing she'd wanted to tell him, and it took him by surprise even more than the first.

He couldn't keep from glancing down at her stomach, which was hidden beneath her coat. Even without the coat, there hadn't been any sign of her being pregnant when he'd stood beside her in the dining room at Vance Hotel. Then again, he hadn't really paid too much attention to her midsection.

As though seeing the direction of his gaze, she pressed a hand to her stomach above her coat. "I'm about five months along."

This situation was growing more confusing by the second. Thatcher had started exchanging letters with her back in early July, which meant her husband had been gone since at least then, if not earlier. That meant she had to be further along than five months.

He wanted to question her about dates and conception and gestation and all those details. He'd learned to be proficient at such things—had to be when he was helping with the mating of livestock as well as pregnancy care and birthing.

But this was neither the time nor place to question her timing and try to help her establish a better due date. The fact was, she was having a baby, and she needed a husband now more than ever.

"Why didn't you tell me in your letters?"

"I didn't know I was with child until after I sent the last one."

He supposed that made sense. But he still didn't understand why she'd chosen to use an alias in her letters. Had she done so just with him? Or had she done it with the other men too? And why? Was she in some kind of trouble?

She was watching him with guarded eyes.

Did it really matter? As she'd said, she'd favored him above the other two men she'd been writing to. Now she was here—better late than never.

"I'm sorry I didn't tell you right away in the dining

room about the baby." She glanced back at the road that led to town. "I wanted to, but it was a private matter, and there were so many people."

"It *was* crowded and busy."

"I'll give you an annulment if you want it."

"No, of course not." He wanted to stay married to her, didn't he, even though she was carrying another man's child?

She was silent a moment. Did she sense his question? His hesitation?

This was a big decision, especially because she was already well along in the pregnancy and there would likely be no way to hide the fact that the baby wasn't his. Not that she would want to hide it. Either way, they would have to tell everyone she was a widow and that the child belonged to another man.

What would people think?

He blew out a tight breath.

"I'm sorry," she said again. "If you want me to go back to town, I won't blame you."

"You're not getting rid of me that easily." He tried to make his voice light to take away some of the seriousness of her confession.

"Thank you, Thatcher. I could tell from your letters you were a kind man, and you've shown that tonight in many ways already."

Something about the way she referred to the kindness

made him wonder if she'd been treated poorly in the past, as if kindness wasn't something she was accustomed to. Had her previous husband been unkind to her?

He'd thought they'd talked about the most important aspects of their lives in their letters, but she'd held things back from him. He supposed that was natural to some extent. How could anyone really get to know another person through just a few letters?

He had a sudden need to know more about her and her past marriage. Her ex-husband's death had to have been recent, maybe in the spring or early summer. Was she still grieving the loss? Or had she been able to move on because she needed someone to take care of her and the baby?

The baby certainly added a dimension to his life and their marriage that he hadn't anticipated. But he was past ready to have children and a family of his own. That was another reason he'd been looking forward to having his mail-order bride come—so that he could start a family. Now it appeared he would have that family sooner than expected.

"I hope you know I didn't set out to deceive you." She was watching him again, probably trying to gauge how he was feeling.

"I know. Finding a partner through a marriage advertisement isn't foolproof. There are bound to be mix-ups and miscommunications. Right?"

"I agree."

"Then let's move forward and make the best of the situation."

"Really?" Her question was filled with disbelief, as if what he was suggesting was too good to be true.

"Really." He still had lots of questions about everything, but he didn't want to pester Eileen—Amelia—for more answers right now. They could sort out the confusion another time.

At the pounding of horse hooves coming from the south, he shifted in his saddle and raised the lantern in the direction of the rider. From the small size, the rider appeared to be a lad.

"Mr. Hoyt?" The voice that rang out was definitely that of a boy and not a man.

Thatcher lifted a hand in greeting. "I'm here."

As the horse thundered closer, Thatcher could see the boy was about ten or twelve years of age.

"I need your help!" the boy called out.

Thatcher was used to emergencies with animals and having to go out at all times of the day or night. It was just one of the realities of being a veterinarian. "What can I do for you?"

The lad brought his horse to an abrupt halt. The light shone upon his face, revealing pale skin and freckles and red hair curling out from beneath a knit cap.

Thatcher was good at remembering names and

people, and he hadn't ever seen the boy before.

Streaks of tears glistened on his cheeks, and his eyes were filled with panic. "My dog is in labor and having lots of trouble. My ma says she's gonna die." The words rushed out all in one breath and ended on a sob.

"Hold on now." Thatcher spoke in a calm tone that he'd perfected for moments like this.

"Can you come out to our place, Mr. Hoyt?" More tears dribbled down the lad's cheeks. "Please come and try to save Bitsy."

"Of course I will." He could do nothing less. "Let me take my wife to our cabin, get my bag—"

"There ain't time. Bitsy's already been in labor for hours, and she's awful weak now."

"It won't take me but a few minutes—"

"Please!" The boy's cry held a note of desperation.

"Where's your bag?" Amelia asked, already veering her horse down the lane.

"In the cabin."

She nudged her horse into a gallop. "Let's get it and go with the boy."

Thatcher watched, trying to make sense of her instructions. She surely didn't mean she wanted to come with him. She had to be tired after her day of traveling.

"Wait here," he said to the lad. Then he kicked his horse into a charge after her. He didn't catch up to her until they reached the cabin. Even then, she was already dismounting. As she started toward the front door of the cabin, she glanced at him over her shoulder. "Where is your bag?"

"By the door." He hopped down and jogged after her. "But you don't need to go with me."

"I want to," she replied as she reached the door and lifted the latch.

As she swung the door open, he stepped past her and found the big brown leather satchel right where he'd left it on the long kitchen table, which was messy with everything he threw there whenever he came home—newspapers, mail, keys, and other miscellaneous items.

He swiped up the bag already stocked with most of what he needed for his calls.

Amelia waited at the door. "Do we need anything else?"

He halted beside the table. "I'm sure you're tired and would like to unpack and get settled in."

"No, I really would like to ride with you." Her pretty features held an earnestness that was difficult to resist. "If it wouldn't be too much trouble."

"It's no trouble . . ."

"Good, then let's go." She disappeared outside.

A moment later, as he closed the door, she was already at her horse and untying her bags from the back.

He knew he should insist on her staying home, warming up, and resting, but a part of him was secretly thrilled she wanted to be with him, or at the very least be a part of his work.

As he reached her, she was tossing her bags to the ground. He made a step with his hands and boosted her back into her saddle. "Hurry," she said as she gathered her reins. "We have to save the dog."

At her use of the word *we*, he almost smiled. He wasn't sure how much knowledge a domestic servant would have about saving a dog in labor, but her presence wouldn't hurt anything. And no doubt about it, he would enjoy the company.

Amelia knelt on the kitchen floor beside Thatcher and the struggling dog. She knew about birthing animals, had always helped her father with calving season and had also witnessed their few sheep and goats give birth.

Birthing was birthing, whether a calf, sheep, goat . . . or dog.

But this situation was obviously precarious. As they'd stepped through the back door and into the kitchen a few moments ago, it had been clear the dog—a mutt that was a mix of sheepdog and Lab—was suffering and wouldn't make it if they didn't help her soon.

Thatcher rubbed a hand over the creature's taut abdomen.

Amelia brushed aside the tail to reveal the dampness of the old blanket she was lying on. "She's lost a lot of fluid."

Thatcher glanced up at her, his eyes rounding.

He had really blue eyes. She hadn't paid attention to their color earlier, had only noticed the kindness reflected in them. But now, up so close, it was hard not to admire the blue that was like a happy, cloudless summer sky with so much potential and promise.

"Is she going to make it?" Across from them, the boy—Stan—was kneeling and stroking Bitsy's head. Although his face was still creased with anxiety, he'd wiped away his tears as they'd ridden up the path to his family's home on the hill above Breckenridge, near one of the mines where his pa worked as a foreman.

The house looked fairly new from the outside, with clean white paint, but the yard was overgrown and dirty, with heaps of broken barrels, iron beams, and other scrap metal. The inside was crowded too, with an assortment of blackened pots and pans, a couple of washing bins and boards, baskets filled with sewing notions, and more.

They'd had to push aside the clutter in order to have room to tend to the dog.

A woman with a toddler on her hip stood in the doorway that led to a hallway. She'd introduced herself as the boy's ma, but Amelia couldn't remember the woman's name. She was lucky Stan's name had stuck.

His ma had been leery about letting them in, announcing right away that she had no money to pay Thatcher for his services. He'd waved off the concern and told her not to worry, that he'd do what he could to help and that she—or Stan—could pay him in whatever way they saw fit.

There was no sight of the pa. Was he working this late? Or was he down on Main Street at one of the many saloons she'd seen on her way out of town earlier?

Stan was watching Thatcher and waiting for his pronouncement on whether Bitsy would live or die.

If Amelia had to make the prognosis, she'd say that Bitsy had no energy or stamina left. The poor dog was nearly comatose, probably from being in labor for so long, losing so much water, and suffering the pain.

Thatcher gently palpated Bitsy's abdomen, swollen like a cow's udder before milking time. "Let's see if we can revive her. If we can't, I'll try a cesarean section."

It was Amelia's turn to look at Thatcher with surprise. He wouldn't really try a cesarean section here on the dirty floor of a mining family's kitchen, would he?

"It would only be a small incision," he replied, clearly sensing her question, "and easy enough to stitch up when I deliver the pups."

She opened his leather bag. "Tell me what to do, and I'll help any way I can."

"There's something blocking her." Thatcher shrugged out of his suit coat, then began rolling up the sleeves of a clean white dress shirt, one that should stay clean and spotless and free of the stains that were sure to come during the delivery. Clearly the animal was more important to him than clothing, and she could respect that about him.

"Maybe one of the pups is facing the wrong way," she suggested.

"That's what I'm thinking. Or maybe the presenting pup is just too big." He finished with one sleeve and then began on the other, revealing strong, tanned arms with flexing muscles. "If you could locate the thermometer in my bag, I'd be obliged. Then, if you don't mind, you could bring me some clean water and soap."

She dug through the satchel that contained a hodgepodge of utensils, medicines, salves, and powders, along with bandages and thread and other supplies. Then with Stan's help, she located warm water in the kettle on the back of the stove and brought a basin of it to Thatcher along with a bar of soap.

He finished taking Bitsy's temperature, then plunged his hands in the basin, lathered them with soap, and began an internal examination. "Yes, I can feel the pup's snout. It's facing the wrong way and clogging things up."

"Do you need forceps?" She'd seen the scissor-like tool in his bag.

He shook his head, his expression turning grave. "Using them would probably harm the puppy, and I think it's still alive."

"Good."

Stan was kneeling across from them again, his eyes

bouncing back and forth between them during their exchange.

Thatcher bit his lip as he focused on what he was feeling inside Bitsy. "I've got the pup's jaw."

Bitsy lifted her head and turned her pitiful eyes upon Thatcher. She was miserable, but at least she was interacting and not so listless.

"Come on, Bitsy." Stan leaned in and crooned gently to the dog. "You can do this, girl."

The mother dog's tail thumped just once against the dirty blanket. It was enough to know that Bitsy loved the boy and would fight for him.

Amelia held the towel toward Thatcher to have at the ready. He leaned in low and appeared to be tugging at the pup slowly. Amelia couldn't see much past his large hand, but the sinews in his arms flexed hard, showing his restraint.

He was obviously a very skilled veterinarian and cared about both the people and their animals. She liked that she was getting to see him in the throes of a crisis. It was the perfect way to judge someone's real character qualities, and she could see that he worked well under pressure, was decisive, a quick thinker, and calm.

"There you are," he said softly as he continued to gently maneuver the pup.

He'd also taken the news about her name confusion and about the baby better than she'd expected. She'd expected him to feel deceived or to question her honesty and morals. But he hadn't been upset, had understood that exchanging a few letters hadn't been enough to get to know each other's situations, and had been willing to continue on with their marriage.

So far, Thatcher was the complete opposite of Charles in just about every way, and she was relieved and grateful to put that part of her past behind her. She could have a new life with a new husband who was respected in the community for his goodness instead of despised for his cheating and lying.

"It's coming now." Thatcher's tone took on a note of excitement. He glanced at Stan. "Let's see if we can get Bitsy to do her part again and push."

Stan rubbed the dog's head. "Come on, girl."

Amelia gently scratched the dog's back. "Let's go, mama. Push that baby out."

They worked together for long moments, encouraging and petting her. Finally, as though realizing her puppy was about to be born, Bitsy grunted and began to make small efforts at helping.

"And there it is." Thatcher guided a wet bundle of fur and mucus out. As he held the pup in his broad palm, the creature didn't move.

Had it died?

Thatcher leaned forward and placed the creature on the rug in front of Bitsy's head. The mother dog eyed the baby wearily but then lifted her head and began to lick it methodically and thoroughly.

In less than thirty seconds, the pup squirmed and then opened its tiny mouth to take a breath.

Stan was still scratching Bitsy's head and crooning words of praise. Thatcher returned to catch another pup, because without the breech puppy holding up the process, the others were coming much more easily.

Three more pups were born, and by the end, Bitsy was busy taking care of them all. Although a little slow, she seemed to be regaining her energy now that her ordeal and the pain were behind her.

After the birthing, Thatcher washed up, and Amelia helped put away the supplies. Thatcher didn't seem in a hurry to leave, and he sat with Stan and the puppies and helped them get started with nursing. All the while he gave Stan advice about how to take care of the puppies, how to train them, and even how to look for homes for them when they were old enough to be weaned.

Stan's ma made them tea and offered them biscuits with homemade strawberry jam, and they sat on the floor with their snack and watched the puppies with Bitsy while Thatcher shared other more daring birthing stories.

Amelia could see Thatcher enjoyed the socializing as much as he'd enjoyed the successful birthing. Even though she was naturally a quieter person who didn't have a lot to say most of the time, she realized she wasn't in a hurry to go either.

Before marrying Charles and moving to Albany, she'd been alone on the farm with her father for so many years. Of course, they'd gone to church, and she'd attended a small country school for a while whenever she could. They'd socialized once in a while with neighbors, and over recent years she'd had some callers—men who'd wanted to court her but hadn't wanted to settle down on the dairy farm with her and Father.

The truth was, she'd led a very lonely and isolated life with just her and Father after Mother had left them. Amelia had forgotten, maybe hadn't ever known, what it was like to sit and talk with people and get to know them.

When Stan's pa finally stumbled inside the front hallway, wavering and slurring and inebriated, Thatcher offered to help carry the man up to bed. But with embarrassment lining their faces, Stan and his ma said they would take care of things and that it was best for Thatcher and Amelia to leave.

The air was colder on the ride out of the hills. Or maybe Amelia was just warmed inside from the beauty of the birthing and even from the tea. Whatever the case, she was glad for the brisk pace Thatcher kept for their ride home. It made talking more difficult, but Thatcher still managed to carry on a conversation about the drinking problem in the mining community and how the temperance movement was gaining ground in Summit County.

When they turned onto the lane that led to his cabin, Amelia was fighting to keep her teeth from chattering. By the time they reached the cabin, she could hardly dismount for the stiffness of her limbs. As Thatcher reached her side and assisted her to the ground, she could no longer hold back the shivering.

His brow furrowed as he took her in. "You're freezing."

"I admit, I'm cold."

He fingered her coat. "You need a heavier winter coat."

"Perhaps I do." She'd left behind the heavier coat she'd worn on the farm in the winter because it had been so bulky and she'd had such limited room in her valises. Now she wished she had brought it.

Thatcher placed a hand on her back and steered her toward the cabin. "Let's get you inside."

She shuffled forward, still shaking.

"Here, let me help." Before she could protest, he swung her up into his arms and was carrying her to the cabin, somehow managing to handle the lantern.

"I can walk." Her protest came out sounding weak.

"Yes, but you're so frozen that you're walking at the pace of a snowman."

"I didn't know snowmen could walk."

"Exactly."

She glanced up to find him grinning at his own jest.

He had nice even teeth when he smiled, which he did freely and frequently. The smiles and humor were as foreign to her as the socializing and conversations.

Her father had rarely smiled and never jested about anything. They'd gotten along just fine without any conflict. And they'd sat together most evenings, reading the newspaper aloud, then playing checkers before going to bed early since they'd had such early mornings. However, their home had always been quiet, somber, and sometimes even sad.

When she'd married Charles and moved into his house, life had grown even more isolated for her, especially as it became clear how much the community disliked Charles. She'd had long days with little to do, and being away from her father and the farm and everything she loved about it had been especially difficult.

Whatever the case, the first evening with Thatcher was proving to be very different from everyone and everything she'd known. And she liked it. She liked him.

He didn't break his steady stride as he carried her to the cabin. When he reached the door, he somehow managed to get it open. He carried her inside, went directly to the closest sofa, and lowered her to the cushion. As he placed the lantern on an end table, he grabbed a blanket off the back of the couch and draped it over her.

"Better?" he asked, glancing around the room, his

gaze landing on another blanket on a chair positioned near the fireplace. He swiped that one and laid it over the first blanket before tucking both blankets around her body more securely.

When he finished, he straightened, then stood back and examined his efforts. "That should tide you over until I get the fire going."

"It will do just fine."

He was already setting to work adding fuel to the remains of a previous fire on the hearth. Within seconds, he had a blaze going. "There."

"Nice work." It would take a few minutes for the cabin to warm up, especially because it was wide open with a loft above the main room.

In addition to the sofa and a couple of chairs on one side, a cast-iron stove and a large table with benches took up the other half of the room. It had a few simple rugs and decorative pillows and curtains. But with the clutter and disarray spread throughout, it was also easy to see that a bachelor had been living there for months.

"Sorry it's so messy," he said, as if he'd read her thoughts.

"It's a cozy place." From what she could tell, except for the main room and loft, there was only one other room—a bedroom.

The bedroom.

She shuddered again.

Thatcher hurriedly struck a match.

Yes, she was still chilled, but more than that, she had nothing but distaste for what was to come.

She'd forgotten all about the wedding night over the past few hours of helping Thatcher deliver the litter of puppies. But the fact was, she was a married woman again, and she was no longer naïve, as she'd been after the short wedding ceremony with Charles. She might not have known exactly what to expect that first night with him, but she knew now.

Of course, a man like Thatcher would probably be more considerate. At least, she hoped so. Either way, she hadn't enjoyed sharing a bedroom or bed with Charles, and she wouldn't ever enjoy that with Thatcher either.

As he added more fuel, a scratching at the door was followed by a resounding bark. She guessed Rusty, his dog, had come to say hello.

Thatcher crossed to the door. "I'll go take care of the horses while—"

She started to push up but stopped when he frowned in her direction.

"—you stay and get warm."

"But I want to help."

He paused with a hand on the door. "I appreciate that. But you need to thaw out so you don't turn permanently into a block of ice."

Before she could protest any further, he stepped

outside and latched the door behind him. Once he was gone, she felt strangely alone. He had such a big and strong presence, but not in an intimidating way. Instead, he was caring and considerate, and she'd enjoyed being with him since the moment they'd left the hotel after the wedding.

She snuggled down under the covers. Maybe the wedding night wouldn't be as bad as she was anticipating. As accommodating as Thatcher had been so far, and after accepting her pregnancy and still being willing to keep her as his wife, he would surely expect her to do her part to make him happy and content.

Yes, she would cooperate with him tonight and every night. It was the least she could do for all he was doing for her.

Thatcher knew he was delaying his return to the cabin, but a strange apprehension held him back.

He paced in front of the barn, the dog lying a few feet away and watching him like he was an idiot. Thatcher had finished unsaddling the horses and tending to them long ago. He'd also fed the sheep and goats and chickens. He'd drawn fresh water from the well and refilled the watering troughs. He'd even brushed Rusty.

Thatcher heaved a sigh of frustration aimed at himself, then paused and stared through the darkness at the outline of the cabin across the yard. The light in the windows beckoned to him.

He wanted to go in and spend time with Amelia, especially after getting to know her throughout the evening and while on his call at the Darwins' to deliver the puppies. She was smart and determined and kind. She'd also been really helpful during the delivery, attentive to his every move and ready to hand him anything he needed, sometimes even before he asked. She hadn't been squeamish and had been more knowledgeable about birthing than he'd expected.

Apparently she'd had more experience with livestock than she'd communicated in her letters. In fact, there seemed to be a lot they hadn't shared with each other.

He began pacing again in the grassy area that was flat and dead and damp after the snowfall last week. He wasn't all that bothered by the new things coming to light about her. As he'd told her, they still had much to learn about each other.

No, that wasn't the problem. The problem was . . . well, he had to clarify their arrangement, particularly for sleeping. His stomach was tying in knots at the prospect of bringing it up, although he didn't know why. It wasn't that hard to tell her he'd like to give them both time to grow comfortable with each other and even develop some affection before sharing the marriage bed.

After all, their relationship hadn't followed the usual pattern of getting to know each other through courtship. So their marriage didn't need to follow the usual pattern of consummating on their wedding night.

But he also didn't know if he should put a timeframe on waiting. Would a month be long enough? Should they wait two? Or should he just leave it open and let feelings develop naturally? If he did that, what if she was never ready? What would he do then? He didn't want to put off marital relations forever.

He'd developed a measure of self-control over the years and had done his best to respect the women who'd come and gone in his life. He hadn't been perfect and had gotten carried away a time or two with women who'd been willing partners, but he'd never been a womanizer. He still wasn't, and he planned to use the same self-control now with Amelia that had held him in good stead in the past.

"You're overthinking this," he whispered. "Just go in there and have an honest discussion about it."

Before he could change his mind—or turn into a coward again—he forced his feet in the direction of the cabin. With his heart pounding, he crossed the distance and entered without stopping, shutting the door firmly behind him and locking it, as though that would somehow force him to stay and talk through their unique marriage situation.

She was on the sofa, where he'd tucked her into the blankets. Both were still wrapped snugly around her body, but she'd lowered herself so that her head now lay on the armrest and her legs were curled up beside her.

At his entrance, she didn't make a move, not even to stir. Had she fallen asleep?

He shrugged out of his duster and hat and hung them on the coat tree beside the door. Then he stepped around the sofa so that he had a better view of her face. Her eyes were closed, and her long lashes rested against her cheeks, which were flushed with a rosy glow—probably a result of the cold breeze during the ride home. Her hair, with its mixture of brown and sun-kissed blond, was still fashionably styled the way it had been for the wedding, but more pieces had come loose and framed her face.

Her expression was peaceful, her breathing even, and her body relaxed beneath the thick layer of blankets. He was glad she could rest easy here. He hoped that meant she trusted him and already felt safe around him.

He watched her, taking advantage of her slumber to study her without her knowing it. As with every time he looked at her face, he was struck by how pretty she was with her gently rounded features, full cheeks, and perfectly curved lips. She was one of those exceptional beauties, the kind of woman who had the power to awe everyone around her.

Why had she ever called herself plain?

He still didn't understand that. Maybe someday he'd ask her and then tell her how wrong she was. But for tonight, he would let her sleep right where she was without disturbing her.

He leaned down and pulled the blankets up to her chin, then wedged them more securely around her.

She stirred and shifted her head but didn't open her eyes and awaken.

When he was certain she was warm and comfortable, he tended to the hearth fire and stove. Minutes later, he crawled into bed, extinguished the lantern on the bedside table, and leaned back, crossing his arms behind his head.

He stared at the ceiling through the darkness, contentedness falling over him. Who would have guessed this morning, as he'd lain in this exact spot feeling lonely and dejected, that by tonight he'd be a married man with a beautiful bride sleeping in the next room?

His pulse kicked up its pace. He was married. Finally. His life was turning around just the way he'd hoped when he'd moved to Colorado. And now he just needed to keep it headed in the right direction.

At a tapping, Thatcher jolted awake out of a deep sleep. Had someone knocked on the door?

He opened his eyes to find the bedroom awash with the light of day. If someone was there, it wouldn't be the first time he'd had a call at dawn. Animals and their problems didn't wait for normal hours. In fact, they seemed to relish getting sick at the oddest times.

At another *tap, tap, tap*, he pushed up to his elbows. Someone *was* at the door.

He threw back the covers, sat up, and glanced

through the open door to the living area. He didn't want anyone to wake Amelia up, so he hastily grabbed his trousers from the floor where he'd dropped them, stepped into them, and yanked them up.

As he stretched one suspender over his long-sleeve undershirt, he stepped out of the bedroom. He was lifting the other suspender but froze at the sight that met him.

Amelia was at the stove, shifting around eggs in one pan before flipping a griddle cake in another. She tapped the wooden spoon against the side of the pan to dislodge the eggs sticking to it with a *tap, tap, tap.*

Maybe the sound he'd heard a moment ago had just been Amelia.

The waft of bacon filled the air along with the scent of freshly brewed coffee. Both made his stomach growl. More than that, the sight of her there at the stove made his heart do a strange flip.

Not only had he been waiting for a moment like this for so long, but she was beautiful even at the early hour, with her hair unbound and falling halfway down her back. Without her coat or the blankets to cover her blouse and skirt, her womanly figure was very much on display through the garments, including a small swell where the baby was growing.

Someday, would he be able to cross over to her, wrap his arms around her from behind, and push aside her curtain of hair to kiss her neck? Would he be able to run his hands over her curvy hips and slide them up her ribs?

At just the prospect of doing so, heat spurted into his bloodstream, but he shook his head to free himself of the lustful thoughts. It was too early in their relationship for him to start thinking about her body and where he'd like to put his hands.

He cleared his throat quietly so that he wouldn't scare her. "Good morning."

She startled anyway, losing hold of the spoon in the eggs. "Oh my." She swiped the spoon back up and seemed to regain her composure before pivoting so that she could take him in—one of his suspenders up and the other now hanging by his side, and his trousers sagging low, revealing part of his underdrawers.

What was he doing standing there so indecently? He fumbled for the suspender and tried to get his fingers to work properly as he shifted the suspender up. On the one hand, there was nothing inappropriate about his appearance since they were married. Even so, she was still mostly a stranger, and he didn't want to overstep himself.

Her gaze lifted to his face and then to his hair. Her eyes rounded before she dropped her attention back to the pan. He caught sight of a smile that she seemed to be trying to hide.

"Go ahead." He combed his fingers through the unruly mop of his wavy hair. "You can laugh. I know I look like a swamp monster when I wake up in the mornings."

"A swamp monster?" She cast him another glance with a widening smile. "Yes, I can see the resemblance."

Fresh warmth spilled through him, but this time bringing a pleasure that was different from the physical attraction he'd just been feeling.

He could get used to this early-morning jesting. He could also get used to seeing her every morning like this, wearing her hair down and cooking in the kitchen.

As though sensing the change in the direction of his thoughts, she dropped her attention back to the pans. "I wasn't sure what time you usually arose, but I always made breakfast for my father at dawn."

"I'll take a hot meal any time you're willing to cook one." He pulled out the closest bench at the table and pushed aside the odds and ends to clear an empty spot. "As long as you promise to eat the meal with me. I'm not the type of man who expects his wife to wait on him like she's a servant."

She stilled.

Had he said something wrong? Maybe the mention of being a servant had come across as critical. "Not that I have anything against young women who are servants. It's just that I believe marriage should be a place where both the husband and wife serve each other."

She flipped another griddle cake. "That's very sweet." Her tone held a note that said she didn't believe it.

"But . . . you don't think it's possible?"

"It's idealistic and hasn't been my experience." She scooped the eggs onto two plates.

He knew he shouldn't pry, but since she'd opened the door to talking about her previous marriage, he wanted to know what it had been like. "Would you tell me about your experience?"

She forked the bacon onto the plates, then added the griddle cakes. She hesitated before turning around and approaching the table with the plates. She set one down before him and the other at the spot across from him. Without a word, she returned to the stove, poured two mugs of coffee, and brought them back to the table.

She sat down, picked up her fork, and took a bite of eggs.

He shrugged and reached for a piece of bacon. "It's all right. I can tell you're not ready—"

"My husband was a loan shark." She ate another forkful of eggs.

Thatcher didn't know much about loan sharks other than that they were known for their shady and often illegal dealings.

She swallowed and then used the edge of her fork to cut off a piece of griddle cake. "I was married to him for less than two months when he was found murdered in his office."

"Murdered?" Thatcher nearly choked on the piece of bacon he was swallowing.

She paused in her eating but didn't look up from her plate. "He was found stabbed in the neck and slumped over his desk."

Thatcher took a sip of coffee to wash down the bacon, then pushed aside his plate, his appetite suddenly gone.

Amelia fiddled around with the food on her fork, then set the utensil down and scooted her plate away too.

He tried to read her face, wanting to see beyond her expression to how she was really feeling. But she was a closed book.

"I'm sorry for your loss," he said tentatively. "I'm sure it was difficult to lose him so soon—"

"Charles wasn't a kind man." The words held a note of bitterness. "Not to me or to anyone."

Thatcher could feel his muscles tightening. "Did he hurt you?"

She hesitated. "He didn't ever hit me. But he was cold and heartless."

Her words should have made him feel better, but they only made him despise the fellow even more. "Why did you marry a man like that?" Charles must have had some redeeming qualities that had attracted her to him.

She took a sip of coffee before finally looking up at him with her hazel eyes. The sadness there nearly took his breath away. "He was planning to foreclose on the farm because my father couldn't repay the loan or the interest. Charles said if I married him, he would forgive my father's loan."

"Did he follow through on that?"

"Yes, at least he honored his word and Father was able to keep the farm."

"Even so, you made a difficult sacrifice."

She set her mug down and twisted it back and forth. "The sacrifice ended up being for nothing. My father died not long after I was married, and Charles sold the farm against my protests."

"Really? That's a horrible thing to do. I'm sorry, Amelia." Thatcher had the urge to stretch across the table and take hold of her hand, but it was too soon to touch her like that, so he reached for his coffee instead.

She focused on her mug, fingering the handle. "My father thought I would be better off with Charles since he was wealthy and had a nice home. He just wanted me to have a safe and secure future."

"He didn't care about Charles's reputation for being cold and heartless?"

"Charles put on a good show for my father and me during those early days of courtship. I had my doubts about Charles but didn't really see him for who he was until after we were married. But I don't think my father ever learned of it—at least, I tried to keep it from him."

"That was noble of you."

She gave a slight shrug. "It didn't work out the way I'd hoped, because without me there to worry about, I think he just gave up."

"What about your mother? And siblings?"

Amelia released a scoffing sound. "I'm an only child. And my mother left my father and me when I was about five."

"Died?"

"No, she went back to New York City, where she was from, said she hated living in the country and wasn't meant to be a mother."

He couldn't relate to that. His own mother had always been sweet and motherly and hadn't wanted him to move so far away. "She sounds selfish."

"To say the least." Amelia took a sip of coffee. "She never once came back. I wrote several letters to her and asked if she would visit. Finally, she responded and told me I was better off without her and not to write to her again."

Thatcher's body was already tense with the indignation over Charles, and now it grew tighter with anger toward this unknown woman. How could any mother be so uncaring and callous? "I guess *selfish* is way too kind of a description."

Amelia's lips quirked into a small smile. "That's true."

He liked that he'd been able to lighten her mood just a little. Maybe Providence had brought her into his life so that he could not just lighten her mood but lighten her life.

"Enough about me and my sad story. Tell me about you." She drew her plate back, picked up her fork, and put a piece of griddle cake in her mouth. As she started to chew, she watched him, clearly waiting for him to share something about himself.

She'd been vulnerable about her past, had been open about her heartache. Could he do the same?

He drew his plate forward and took a bite of eggs. He couldn't tell her about the disastrous end to his veterinary practice in Iowa. Not yet. It was too mortifying. But he could talk about other difficulties he'd experienced, particularly with his family.

"So I told you in one of my letters that I'm from Iowa."

She paused in her chewing and lifted a brow in question. Didn't she remember?

"I wrote that I grew up on a farm outside of Cedar Rapids, the second oldest of five siblings."

She swallowed. "I'm sorry, Thatcher. I don't remember. And I meant to reread your letters when I reached Fairplay, but I lost them somewhere during the journey west."

Something in her tone set him on edge. "Were you in a hurry because you were in trouble?"

She pushed her eggs around on her plate, then met his gaze directly. "I didn't feel safe anymore."

7

Amelia wasn't sure why she was sharing so much personal information with Thatcher. Maybe because he was easy to talk to and was a good listener.

She supposed she also wanted to be honest with him about everything. She didn't have the happiest of pasts, and she didn't have a happy reason for coming west to be his bride. How many mail-order brides did? If they had a happy life, why would they move to a strange place to marry strange men?

"Are you in danger from the murderer?" Thatcher stopped eating his breakfast again and sat forward, his brawny body and muscles rigid.

His blond hair was still sticking up in some places, but he didn't resemble a swamp monster—whatever that was. Instead, he looked endearingly bed tousled, especially with the light shadow of scruff on his face.

"Do you think he'll come after you?" Thatcher continued.

See, this was why she needed to confess everything. She wanted him to know exactly the kind of problems she had so that he could make an informed decision about whether to move forward with their marriage before consummating their union.

Last night she must have fallen asleep while waiting for him to return. She was surprised he hadn't woken her when he'd come in. She wasn't a deep sleeper, and if he'd made any effort to rouse her, she would have heard him.

No, he hadn't disturbed her. In fact, as she'd risen this morning, she'd felt a little guilty that she hadn't made more of an effort to go to him. A part of her had been grateful to him for giving her the time to rest after such a busy day. But she couldn't make that a habit.

She expelled a breath. "The murder suspect was one of the businessmen in Albany that Charles cheated and ruined."

"In Albany and not New York City?"

That was a strange question. Why would Thatcher think she'd lived in New York City? "Charles's office was in Albany. Not only did he provide loans to the farmers in the area, but he also offered loans to businesses in the community."

"More loans with high interest and exorbitant fees?"

"Exactly."

"So this fellow had had enough of Charles and his cheating ways?"

"Mr. Kay lost his dry goods store and, as a result, had to move out of his home above the store. The family moved to a room in a boarding house, and he was working odd jobs to pay for the room. But then over the summer, when two of his children died from measles, his wife had a breakdown and, well . . . she died too." The news of her suicide had spread throughout town, and even though Amelia had been ostracized from the community, she'd still heard about it.

She could feel Thatcher watching her, listening to her carefully. But she didn't sense his condemnation, only his compassion.

"A week later, Charles was murdered."

"And the police found evidence against Mr. Kay?"

"I'm not really sure. They never said anything to me. They came to the house after finding Charles to inform me of his death and to ask a few questions. But that was all."

"So how did you find out it was Mr. Kay? Did he threaten you?"

"No, I never did see him or talk to him. But Charles's brother came to visit from New York City to make the burial arrangements, and he began an investigation." She'd only met Geoff once before Charles died, and she'd disliked him more than Charles—if that were possible. "Eventually, Geoff informed me that his investigator suspected Mr. Kay."

"Did he say why? What proof they had?"

She shook her head. "No, he just warned me I was in danger and should leave, that Mr. Kay was making plans to hurt me too."

"Why wouldn't he have Mr. Kay arrested if the investigator had evidence against him?"

"The truth is, I'm not sure the killer was Mr. Kay. Part of me wonders if Geoff was behind it all."

"Geoff sounds like a snake."

"Oh, he was every bit as much of a snake as Charles. I think Geoff wanted to scare me into going so that I would lose my portion of Charles's fortune, which according to the will, I would forfeit if I left New York."

"Geoff wanted his brother's fortune for himself."

"I didn't want Charles's dirty money, but I also didn't think Geoff deserved it. So even though the community despised me because of Charles—"

"What?" Thatcher's eyes widened with disbelief. "They despised you? How could they? It's easy to see you're a kind and helpful and generous woman."

She could feel her insides warm at his praise. "Thank you. But I was shunned and an outcast from the moment I arrived in town as his bride. No one took the time to get to know me."

"That must have been hard."

"It made me resolve to choose a new husband who is well-respected and held in high esteem—someone like you."

He shifted in his chair, then reached for his coffee, which was no longer steaming, and swigged a mouthful.

"Regardless of what everyone thought of me," she continued her tale, "the day before I left, I withdrew all the money from the bank that I could—most of the fortune—and I tracked down the people Charles had hurt and gave them the money."

"You did?" Thatcher's eyes lit up. "I love it."

"It didn't make up for what Charles had stolen from them, but it was at least something. I kept only enough money to cover my expenses for the trip here, not even equivalent to what my father's farm was worth."

"And what did Geoff think of that?"

"I don't know. I left the next morning before he found out."

"That was probably wise."

She took another bite of her breakfast, which had grown cold. "I didn't feel safe with Geoff to begin with and knew he'd hate me after spending all that money."

"Do you think Geoff will come after you?" Thatcher's expression turned somber. "Maybe hire a detective and hunt you down?"

"I don't think he would go to the trouble." At least, she hoped not. "What reason would he have for doing so? I gave away everything and have nothing now for him to take."

"Maybe for revenge?"

"If he does, I've been going by my maiden name, Stone. Hopefully, that will make his task more difficult."

Thatcher was quiet a moment. "I'm glad you made it here safely."

He wasn't upset? That was all he had to say after she'd aired her dirty linen so openly? If so, he really was a good man. "So does that mean you won't be asking me to leave now that you know the whole truth about me?"

He held her gaze, and the gentleness there seemed to reach across the table and caress her. "I haven't even considered it."

"Not even a little?"

"Why would I?"

She really did like Thatcher. He'd once again listened to her without passing judgment. "Because I obviously came to you with a whole lot more to my history than I disclosed."

"I have a whole lot more to my history too."

"That's right. You were about to tell me about you, and I took over the conversation again."

He lifted his fork and took a big bite of his griddle cake.

Before she could think of a question to ask him, a rapid knock sounded against the door. She startled, sloshing some of her coffee onto the table.

Maybe she was more nervous about Geoff tracking her down than she was admitting to herself. She didn't think he would, but maybe it would just take time to feel confident that she had nothing to worry about anymore.

"Mr. Hoyt?" came a voice from outside.

"Coming," Thatcher called as he pushed back from the table and swung off the bench.

"Mr. Mintz sent me about his mare," the person outside called.

Thatcher started across the room, one of his suspenders down, his big toe showing through a hole in his socks, and his hair still messy.

Before starting breakfast, Amelia had groomed herself as best she could since her bags were both sitting in the main room where Thatcher had delivered them last night. Even so, she hadn't fixed her hair yet and rapidly began winding it up into a knot at the base of her head.

As Thatcher opened the door, daylight spilled inside along with the chill of the early morning.

A young man stood outside on the front stoop, wearing a heavy coat, leather gloves, and a cowboy hat. "Sorry to bother you this early, Mr. Hoyt. But Mr. Mintz said he's putting the horse down this morning."

Thatcher reached for his duster on the coat tree by the door. "Tell Mr. Mintz to wait and let me come take a look at her first. If there's a chance I can save her, I will."

"That's what he said you'd want to do." The man peered past Thatcher toward Amelia as she finished with the last twist of the bun. It wasn't secured by pins, but it would hold until after their visitor left.

Frowning, Thatcher started to close the door. "Tell Mr. Mintz I'll be there shortly."

The man shifted his head in order to continue looking at Amelia until the door shut completely on him.

Thatcher turned around with a frown. "Was he ogling you?" he whispered. "Or was I imagining it?"

"I suppose he was just curious about your new bride."

Thatcher seemed to consider her answer before shaking his head. "No, he was definitely interested in you."

"Well, that doesn't matter, does it?" She began to cross to her bags. "I'm married to you."

He stuffed his arm into his coat sleeve. "So you're all in? No wanting to back out?"

She stopped beside her bag and leveled a look at him. "I'm all in, Thatcher, and I don't want to back out if you're accepting me for . . . well, everything."

"I do accept you." He pulled his duster on all the way. "And I hope you'll do the same for me."

"I will."

His hand on one of his coat buttons grew motionless, and his expression was serious and devoid of any humor. "Things aren't always going to be perfect, and we might second-guess the way our relationship came about once in a while. But to my way of seeing things, we're married and made a binding commitment that I'm not planning to end because of any hardships we face."

"I agree." She sort of felt as though they were saying their wedding vows again, but this time with more meaning now that they'd gotten to know each other a little.

"Good." The tension seemed to ease from his shoulders.

"Good."

His lips curved up into one of his handsome smiles. "Now that we have that settled, I'm afraid I have to go out this morning."

She knelt beside her bag and began to fish inside for her hairpins. "I'd like to go with you."

In the process of grabbing his Stetson and opening the door, he halted. "You would?"

"Yes." She found a pin, used her teeth to help open it, then stuck it into her hair to secure it in place.

He closed the door.

She put another pin in place and could feel him watching each move she made. She glanced his way with a third pin in her mouth. "Is that okay?"

His features were somber. "The mare has foundered. And her hoof won't be pretty to look at."

She slid the last pin in place. "I don't mind."

"If it's too bad, Mr. Mintz will have to shoot her." He positioned the Stetson on his head.

She straightened her shoulders. "I'm not afraid of any

of that, Thatcher. But if you don't want me to go along, I can stay here and unpack—"

"I do want you to go along." His voice held a sincerity that told her he was being honest. "It's just that my job isn't all that glamorous or easy at times."

"I'd still love to see what you do and help you if you need it."

He studied her, slowly taking in her hair, then letting his gaze drop to her bodice and down to her skirt. Was that a glimmer of appreciation in his eyes? Or attraction?

She'd witnessed the shrewd and calculated desire in Charles's eyes and had learned what it meant. But this look in Thatcher's eyes was different. There was nothing lustful about it. Instead, it was more like someone standing at a distance and admiring a sunset with a mixture of awe and satisfaction.

As his gaze lifted and connected with hers, he offered her another smile, one that was genuine, even happy . . . and made him look boyish.

He was already good-looking in his coat and hat, with his scruffy face and broad features. But his smile? It was almost devastating and made her heart do a strange flip—a pleasant flip she'd never experienced before.

"I'll go saddle our horses."

She nodded wordlessly.

When he stepped out, she blew out a breath and then let herself smile. Maybe after all the heartache she'd experienced, she would finally find a home. Was it too much to hope that she could actually enjoy being married to her new husband?

She wasn't expecting a happily ever after. That was too much to ask for. But to have some happiness? Was that within reach?

She hoped so.

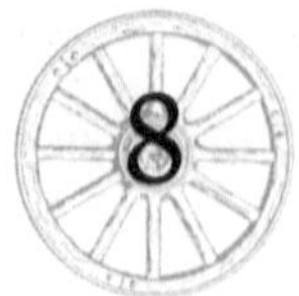

Thatcher gently placed the mare's leg back to the ground, then sighed his frustration. "It's gotten worse."

Standing outside the stall, Mr. Mintz already had his rifle under his arm. "That's what I figured. But you told me to call you first before I put her out of her misery."

Amelia stood beside Thatcher, had been there the whole time he'd examined the bloody hoof. She'd watched without flinching and was now gently rubbing the mare's flank, probably attempting to comfort the black Percheron. The scent of horseflesh and manure lingered heavily in the barn, which was chilly at the early hour, but Amelia didn't seem bothered by that either.

"The mare doesn't have to be put down yet." Thatcher reached into his bag for the ointment he'd put on the wound yesterday. "If you soak her foot a few times a day, keep it clean, and change around her diet, there's still hope for her."

Mr. Mintz shook his head. "I told you I don't have time for pampering a horse like that. I got a business to run."

The young man Mr. Mintz had sent after them stood in the aisle a short distance away. He was still staring at Amelia the same way he had earlier when he'd noticed her at the cabin. Thatcher hadn't liked the fellow paying her attention then, and he still didn't.

Thatcher had wanted to tell him that Amelia was his wife now and he'd better not get any ideas about trying to take her away from him. No one had better.

The jealousy was new to Thatcher and irrational. But he'd done the hard work of getting her to come to the West, and if the fellow wanted a bride, he'd have to do the same.

"What are the mare's chances of healing from this?" Amelia asked quietly.

"It's a long shot," Mr. Mintz replied before Thatcher could. "Even if we go to all the work Mr. Hoyt is suggesting, she still might not get better."

Amelia didn't bother looking at the middle-aged man and instead fixed her attention on Thatcher as he rubbed the ointment into the horse's hoof.

Thatcher wished he could reassure her, but he couldn't. "Mr. Mintz is right. Even with lots of good care, she may never heal."

Amelia raised a hand and stroked the horse's glossy mane.

The lighting in the barn was low, coming from a single lantern hanging from a rafter in the aisle. It illuminated the dozen or so stalls that held Mr. Mintz's other horses and livestock. From Thatcher's count, the man had eight horses. Losing one wouldn't hurt him. Even so, Thatcher never liked to give up on an animal when there was still a chance of saving it.

Mr. Mintz held the rifle out to the young fellow. "Go on, Johnnie, and take the mare out to the corral and shoot her."

"No." Amelia took a step toward the stall door, and her expression turned stormy, as if she planned to wrestle the gun out of their hands.

Mr. Mintz paused.

"I'll doctor her," Amelia said, drawing her coat closed around her—the coat that was too thin. "I'll do all the work to help her, and you won't need to do any."

Thatcher could only stare at her in surprise, the same as the other two men.

"I'll come every day and do everything necessary to doctor her."

Not only was the wound putrid and difficult to look at, but the commitment was enormous for a woman in her condition. In fact, it was probably unrealistic, since initially the horse would need care at least three times a day, if not more. Thatcher wouldn't be able to ride over that often, and he didn't want Amelia to make the trek by herself.

"I don't think that would work—" he started.

"I won't mind the work." Her beautiful eyes pleaded with him.

He dipped his hands into the bucket of nearby water and lathered up with a bar of soap. How could he say no to her when she was looking at him like that and so eager to help? He couldn't. Especially because he didn't want to see the horse put down either. That was why he'd come again, because he wanted to come up with a solution to save the creature.

Maybe he could attempt to take the horse back to his place. She would have trouble walking the distance there, but if he bandaged her hoof with a thick padding and they went slowly, they might be able to do it without hurting her even more.

Would Mr. Mintz agree to it?

He met the man's gaze as he dried his hands. "Would you allow us to walk her back to my farm? If Amelia wants to doctor her and see if she can help, I'd rather her do it there."

Mr. Mintz hesitated a moment before pulling back his rifle. "Don't see any harm in it."

Amelia's hand was taut against the horse's mane. "If we can get her better, we'll bring her back."

"No need." Mr. Mintz tucked his weapon under his arm. "If she lives, you can keep her."

Amelia stroked the horse's muzzle. "I couldn't take her—"

"Mr. Hoyt only has one horse. He'll need another now that he's got you."

Amelia fell silent.

"Besides, I owe Mr. Hoyt for his services—"

"No, it's okay," Thatcher cut in. "I didn't really help—"

"Take her if you want her." Mr. Mintz pivoted and began to stalk toward the barn door. "Otherwise Johnnie's gonna put her down."

Thankfully, Johnnie followed after Mr. Mintz. As soon as they were out of earshot, Amelia leaned in. "Please, Thatcher." Her voice was low and urgent, and her eyes were once again so full of hope. "Could we keep her?"

Her obvious desire to save the horse was unexpected, but he liked it. A lot. He liked her a lot.

"I promise I'll do all the caretaking," she continued.

He lifted a hand and touched her lips to silence her.

She halted her next sentence and watched him with anticipation.

"We'll bring her back and do the caretaking together."

The gold flecks in the hazel of her eyes seemed to

melt, and her lips curved up into a small smile. "Really?"

"Really."

She studied his face, her eyes still warm. "Thank you."

"We'll have a lot of hard work ahead of us and long hours."

"I don't mind."

He shifted his fingers to her cheek, then dropped his hand, knowing he had no right yet to caress her. "Let's get going. It'll take us a while to get her ready to leave, and then the journey home will be hard."

They worked together to bandage the mare's hoof with enough cushion that she could walk on it. Even with the padding, they went at a snail's pace for the several miles home and had to stop twice to redo the bandages and add more cushion.

By the time they reached the barn, the afternoon was half over. They spent the rest of the day tending to the deformed hoof. Thatcher trimmed the flesh and bone as best he could. Then together, they soaked it in water, cleaned it, scoured the stall, and then gathered bland fodder for her to eat.

When her foot was bandaged again and she was resting comfortably, Amelia leaned against the split-rail stall beam and watched while Thatcher examined the other hooves.

The split-log barn was much smaller than the barn on Thatcher's family's land in Iowa. It only had enough room for the wagon, the farming supplies, hay and feed, and the few animals he'd collected. It was also much quieter and, with the fall of darkness, was shadowed.

"She seems content," Amelia said. "But will she get better?"

Thatcher finished with the last hoof and placed it on the ground. "She's young enough that she ought to be able to heal."

"I hope so."

"She's in good hands."

"I agree. You're an excellent veterinarian, Thatcher."

"No, I was talking about you." He braced himself against the railing beside her. "You were patient and gentle and persistent."

Amelia ducked her head, but not before he caught sight of the pleasure on her face.

"I'm not exaggerating. You're really good with the mare."

"Thank you." Amelia kept her focus on the mare, but Thatcher couldn't stop himself from admiring Amelia's profile. With her hair pulled back and the top button of her blouse undone, he glimpsed her neck and collarbone. Her cheeks were full and the dimples always so enticing.

After spending the day with her, he would have thought he'd become more accustomed to her beauty and not feel the draw to look at her every chance he had. But the truth was, instead of being satisfied, he wanted to stare at her even more.

"So, what would you like to name her?"

"Doesn't she already have a name?"

"You saved her, so you get to give her the name you want."

"Is that how it works?" Her voice contained a note of humor.

"Seems fair to me." He studied the horse, who was a big girl, probably because of her inactivity. "She looks like a Pudge to me."

Amelia released a scoffing sound. "With how tall and black she is, I was thinking she's regal and deserves a name like Queen."

"I didn't realize it was that easy to become royalty."

"It's very easy and all about the bearing."

"Then I should qualify." He straightened and struck a haughty, serious pose. Except he was wearing his duster and Stetson and hadn't shaved.

"You look more like one of those crooks on a Wanted poster."

He shifted and lifted a brow at her. "So let me see if I have this right. You think the horse resembles a queen, but I look like a criminal?"

She laughed lightly. "No, that's not what I meant. You could never be a criminal. You're probably the kindest and most perfect man I've ever met."

Perfect? He wasn't perfect. In fact, his record as a

veterinarian was far from stellar.

A flood of memories came rushing back—the sleepless nights, the tireless efforts to help the sick foal, and the fire sweeping through the barn and destroying everything.

Should he confess his past to her now? The devastating fire that had started because of his carelessness and destroyed some of the finest horses that had ever lived. And he hadn't been able to do one thing about it.

He wasn't a *wanted* man. No, he was *un*wanted. He'd tarnished his reputation so badly that no one had wanted him around. No one had trusted him. No one had believed in him.

Thankfully, here in this wild land, he'd been given a second chance.

"I'm not perfect, Amelia," he finally said softly. "I wish I were. But I have plenty of faults."

She was quiet a moment, as though realizing the shift in the conversation to a more serious nature. "We all have faults."

He had to tell her now about the mistakes he'd made, the problems he'd caused. She deserved to know all about him the same way he now knew all about her.

She also deserved to know that being married to a man like him came with risks. Although everyone in Breckenridge and Summit County liked him now, the tide could turn all too easily. One wrong move, and he could become an outcast again overnight.

She'd already been married to one outcast, and she didn't need the risk of being married to another.

He opened his mouth to say more, but she released a noisy yawn before he could confess his sordid tale.

"You're tired." He straightened and wanted to palm his forehead for his insensitivity toward her. She was with child and needed to rest more frequently as well as have proper nutrition. But she'd been on her feet all day, and they hadn't eaten anything since their half-touched breakfast that morning. "We should call it a day."

"I admit, I am growing tired." She stifled another yawn.

Before he could think through his actions, he swept her up off her feet and began to carry her.

She stiffened. "What are you doing?"

He was winding his way through the barn. "I'm guilty of allowing you to do too much today, and now I can't let you do one more single thing, not even walk."

She gave a huff of a laugh. "I'll be fine, Thatcher."

"You'll be fine once you're resting on the sofa."

She wiggled, probably in an effort to make him put her down.

But now that he had her, he situated her more securely. "Just relax," he said softly, bending close to her ear, "and let me do this. It might not help you, but it'll help me feel better about being such an idiot for not considering your needs."

She laughed again and settled against him, no longer fighting his hold.

As he carried her the rest of the distance, he tried not to think about how she felt in his arms—so soft and supple and sensual. But his nerves were attuned to every pressure point of her body touching his—the way strands of hair brushed his chin, the slender stretch of her arm around his neck, the gentle curve of her body against his chest, and the firmness of her backside draped over his arm.

Her face was also close, and he could feel the warmth of her breath whenever she bantered back with him during the short walk to the cabin. When he entered, he deposited her on the sofa as he'd done the previous night.

Of course she protested, but as he lit the hearth fire, he convinced her to let him warm up an easy supper of the griddle cakes left from breakfast along with a can of pork and beans. When the meal was ready, he brought her plate to the sofa and pulled up a chair to the fireplace for himself. They ate and talked, and he told her more about the German immigrant family who had built the home and settled the land—how the mother had died and the father of two little children had ended up murdered and an estranged brother had come from Germany to visit, only to find the children living with a neighbor woman. Everyone claimed the estranged brother had fallen in love at first sight with the neighbor woman.

Whether he had or not, he'd married the woman within just a couple of weeks and taken her and the children back to Germany with him.

Love at first sight. Thatcher wasn't sure if that could really happen, but the love story of the previous residents of the cabin took on new meaning as he considered his relationship with Amelia and how long it might take for love to bloom between them.

As Thatcher relaxed with her in the low light and the cozy warmth, he found himself feeling more content than he'd been in a long time. This was the kind of life he'd wanted, the companionship and friendship he'd been missing. It was actually better than he could have asked for because she'd spent the day with him, joining in his work and assisting him, and he'd loved every minute of their time together.

When he left her to check on the livestock and Queen, he raced through the chores, eager to return to Amelia. Only as he stepped back through the door a while later did he remember that he still hadn't had that conversation with her about the marriage bed. He couldn't put it off another night.

No, he had to offer her the bed, and he would sleep up in the loft . . . just until they both felt more comfortable with each other, whenever that might be. But as he approached the sofa and found her in a deep sleep, he covered her securely with the blankets again, banked the fire, and turned out the lantern.

He would sleep a final night in the bedroom. By tomorrow night, he would be in the loft, and he'd make sure she had the bed. That meant he had to talk to her about the marriage bed tomorrow, no matter how awkward the conversation would be.

Amelia awoke to darkness. She stretched to the warmth of the blankets on top of her and the sofa cushions beneath.

That meant she'd fallen asleep again before Thatcher had returned from the barn. She hadn't wanted to, had tried to keep her eyes open . . . mostly for an update on Queen's condition. But maybe a small part of her had wanted to talk with Thatcher again too.

She'd actually wanted to go out to the barn with him and tend to Queen one last time for the night. But Thatcher had insisted she remain inside and rest. She'd acquiesced, mostly because she had been exhausted and because she had to take care of herself for the baby's sake.

She pushed up to a sitting position. The glow of a low fire provided some light, as did the glimmer from the stove. Through the open door of the bedroom, she could see the outline of Thatcher's boots and trousers on the floor, where he'd discarded them before climbing into bed.

He was sleeping alone for a second night in a row. He couldn't be happy about it, not after how excited everyone had claimed he was to get married. Of course, there were probably lots of reasons why he was excited. But as a man, he would be wanting to have his needs met. There was no getting around it.

She flopped back to the couch and stared at the dark outline of the ceiling beams overhead. She could go on ignoring Thatcher, pretending the marriage bed didn't exist and putting it off as long as possible.

But what would be the point of that? She would eventually need to fulfill her marital duties.

Huffing out a breath, she sat back up. She might as well do her part. After all, he'd been so kind to her—had taken her in, had agreed to raise her child, and was providing for her every need. Withholding herself from him would make her seem ungrateful and selfish and uncooperative.

She pushed off the blankets and swung her feet over the edge of the sofa. As her stocking feet touched the floorboards, the draft as well as the coldness of the boards made her shiver. But she stood and shuffled toward her bags.

She dug around inside and found her nightgown. It wasn't a heavy wool one like she'd had on the farm. No, it was a thin, silky gown that was cut low, one that Charles had given her after throwing away all her others.

The revealing gown wouldn't be warm enough for the winter nights ahead. But she had nothing else now, and it would have to do.

She changed rapidly, then wrapped herself up in one of the blankets from the sofa before tiptoeing past the table. She halted in the bedroom doorway, a nervous tremor racing through her.

Of course, she'd been nervous on her wedding night with Charles as well as curious and maybe even a little scared.

But this nervousness was different. Because the truth was, she already liked Thatcher much more than she ever had Charles. And she didn't want to disappoint him tonight. She wanted him to like her too, and she wanted him to be happy that he'd chosen to marry her.

She adjusted the thin straps of the nightgown, pulling the material up so that she wasn't showing so much cleavage, which was difficult because God—and her mother—had given her a curvy bust.

Although the bedroom was dark, her eyes adjusted within seconds, and she could distinguish Thatcher's form taking up most of the bed. He was sprawled out on his back, with both his legs and arms tangled in the covers.

She couldn't see his handsome face, but it was easy to view his muscular limbs and brawny build. The sight of his body brought back the memory of how he'd carried her to the house again with such ease and tenderness, yet also with such strength.

Yes, there was something different in the physical tug she was feeling toward Thatcher, something she'd never felt with Charles, probably because she'd never liked him as a person. Maybe if he'd been caring and had made an effort to get to know her, she might have felt more of a tug toward him too.

Whatever the case, she wasn't dreading joining Thatcher in bed. Instead, more of that nervousness tingled inside her stomach. She flattened a hand there, and then before she lost the courage, she silently crossed to the bed.

What should she do? Slip under the covers beside him and wait for him to wake up? Surely her movement would rouse him. Hopefully she wouldn't need to say anything for him to know why she was there. And hopefully they wouldn't have to talk about their nighttime activities in the morning and could pretend nothing had happened. She liked their relationship so far and didn't want things to become awkward between them.

Steeling herself, she dropped the blanket from her shoulders, letting it puddle on the floor next to his trousers. Then she folded the covers down enough that she could slide first one foot underneath and then the other.

As she lowered her whole body onto the mattress, the

chill in the unheated room skimmed across her scantily clad body. Sinking down and stretching out, she tugged at the covers to free them from his limbs and brought them up the rest of the way over her body, all the way to her chin.

She lay rigidly, without moving. Even though the sheets were cool, she could feel the warmth radiating from his body. He was only inches away, but he didn't move either. Not even a change in his steady and even breathing.

She waited and listened again. He continued to slumber undisturbed, just as peacefully as when she'd first stepped up to the bedroom doorway, probably unaware that she was in bed. Maybe she would have some time to ease her way into the situation and get comfortable lying beside him before he woke up and reached for her.

Drawing in a breath, she tried to calm her racing heart. She didn't need to be afraid. Hadn't Thatcher proven himself to be a man of character in every way so far? She'd never met a man quite like him before, so well-liked by everyone in the community.

As nice as he was, if she kept from awakening him, maybe she could have another night of freedom. In the meantime, she would show him that she wasn't the one holding back and that she was willing to sleep with him.

Long minutes passed, and when he still didn't awaken, she let herself begin to relax. As her eyes adjusted to the darkness, she took in the room, which was only big enough to hold the bed, a narrow chest of drawers, and a trunk. There was very little room to maneuver, but it was cozy and private, and that's all that really mattered.

She shifted slightly so that she was reclining on one side, facing Thatcher. She was close enough that, even through the shadows, she could still see his features—the strong lines of his jaw, his broad chin, his well-defined nose, and his deep eyes.

Her heart gave a stuttering patter, and she had the unusual urge to lift her hand and trace every handsome line of his face.

Should she make the first move? What would he think of her if she did?

With a soft exhale, she returned to her back and lifted her gaze to the ceiling again. No, it was much safer if she kept to herself. She'd done her part and made herself available to him. Now the next move was up to him.

As her eyes grew heavy again, she finally shut them. Thatcher was no threat to her. In fact, now that she was next to him in the bed, a sense of security fell over her. She was in a safe place, she was on the cusp of a new life, and maybe she could rest easily for the first time in months.

10

Something warm and soft pressed against Thatcher in his dreams, something he didn't want to let go of.

The dream was about Amelia, as all of his dreams had been since their wedding. But this one was more realistic than any of the others, almost as if he could really touch her and feel her body against his.

It was a dream too good to be true, and he simply wanted to bask in the oblivion for a moment longer.

But something wiggled against his bare leg.

His eyes flew open to the darkness of the bedroom that told him it wasn't yet dawn. He started to roll over only to find that his leg was actually trapped underneath . . . another leg.

Wakefulness crashed into him, bringing every nerve in his body to full attention and making him aware of not only the leg draped over his but a body curled up against his side and a face next to his on the pillow.

Amelia. He knew it was her right away, didn't even have to think for a second.

He sucked in a breath and pinched his eyes closed. What in the name of all that was holy was she doing in bed with him?

She stirred, stopped breathing, then began to carefully inch away from him.

She must have been asleep and had now woken and was trying to put a proper distance between them. But she obviously hadn't realized he was awake too, or she wouldn't be moving so covertly.

As she tried to back away, he became more conscious of her body against his. He hadn't been dreaming after all. She really had been next to him, her warm and soft body pressed to his. In fact, she was still mostly against him—he could feel the length of her.

Had she been cold? Was that why she'd gotten into bed with him? Maybe the blankets on the sofa hadn't been enough and she'd needed his body heat.

Whatever the case, she'd been much bolder than he'd expected. Much bolder than he was. Was that because she'd already been married? She had no reason to be a prude. Not when they had every right to share a bed now that they were man and wife.

Even if she'd been daring enough to crawl in beside him, her actions now in trying to extricate herself told him she hadn't meant to take things quite so far.

As she slid her leg off his and down to the mattress, he knew he needed to make her aware that he was awake. He didn't want to deceive her into thinking he was still sleeping, and he may as well have that talk with her about waiting for intimacy.

She began to slide back even more, putting some distance between their bodies. That was probably for the best. But as soon as the soft pressure of her body was gone, he immediately wanted it back. He almost reached for her, but he restrained himself and lay motionless until she was a hand's distance from him.

Only then did he release a tight breath.

At his exhale, she stiffened. "Thatcher?" she whispered.

"I'm awake."

"How long?"

"A minute or two."

She made a frustrated sound. "I'm sorry for bothering you. I didn't mean to get so close. I must have been cold. I apologize—"

"It's all right."

"No, really. I didn't mean to crowd your space—"

"Amelia." He somehow managed to touch her lips with his fingers and silence her. He couldn't see her features clearly, but it was light enough that he could see the outline of her face and knew she was looking at him and trying to read his expression. "There's nothing to apologize for."

She fell silent, her lips closing beneath his fingertips—her soft but full lips that he had kissed at their wedding very briefly. The kiss had only given him a small taste of her sweetness. But he'd determined to be patient with kissing her every bit as much as he wanted to be patient with the marriage bed.

If he wasn't extra careful in this current situation, he would jump right over a line he didn't want to cross yet. That meant he had to take his fingers away from her lips—lips that were puckered from her protest, the curve alluring, the softness so inviting.

His muscles tensed, but somehow he managed to move his hand away from her mouth and back to his side.

"I'm sorry if I startled you." She whispered another apology. "But I didn't want you to think I was trying to avoid . . . this."

Avoid what? "I wasn't thinking that . . ."

"You weren't?" Her whisper held a note of surprise.

What was she talking about? He was growing more confused by the second.

"Then you're not upset at me?"

Her head was still on his pillow, only inches from his. "Of course not. Why would I be upset?"

"For . . . you know . . . falling asleep on the sofa and not being awake to . . ."

His whirling mind came to an abrupt halt. Was she

insinuating she'd come to bed with him because she thought he would be angry about not being with her? Had he given her that impression?

He hoped not.

He released another tight breath. He should have had the conversation about expectations by now. If he'd been more proactive, they wouldn't be in this awkward position.

He rolled over to his back and stared at the ceiling. He had to say something now.

Before he could formulate a sentence, she spoke first. "You're doing your duty to me to take care of me and my unborn child. I'd like to do my duty to you."

"Duty?"

"Yes, you know." Her voice was matter-of-fact. "I won't stop you from exercising your husbandly rights."

"Whoa, now." He sat up and began to scramble off the end of the bed. The conversation was going downhill fast. *Duty. Husbandly rights.* He knew exactly what she was insinuating, that he could have his way with her and she wouldn't stop him. The very idea of sating his needs with her like she was his possession was repulsive.

As his feet hit the floor, the coldness of the floorboards jarred him awake even more. She'd come to his bed because she thought it was expected of her. Maybe she even thought it was a way to repay him.

With a huff, he paced to the door, then halted. He

couldn't just walk away and leave her in the bed. "Amelia, it's not like that. I'm not like that." He turned back around to face her.

She was sitting up, the covers pushed aside and revealing her night clothing—if it even could be called clothing with how scanty it was. Even through the darkness, the miles of her pale, bare skin were visible. Except for thin straps, her shoulders, arms, and neck were completely uncovered. The lacy edge dipped low, revealing the gentle swell of her bust. The skirt had bunched up above her knees, leaving her legs visible.

His mouth went suddenly dry even as his heart began to pound a strange, wild tempo. She was a very desirable woman. There was no sense in denying it. In fact, the more he took her in, with her long hair flowing all around her, dangling over her shoulders, draping over her back, the harder and faster the drum inside his chest beat.

This was his wife. She was in his bed. And she was a willing partner. Why should he deny himself if she was ready to consummate? If they did, then he wouldn't have to worry about anyone questioning the legitimacy of their marriage.

He shook his head and dropped his gaze away from her. "This isn't the way I want it to be between us." The words came out low and hoarse.

She was silent.

He jammed his fingers through his messy hair, which

was already sticking up in disarray. "I meant to tell you that I want to wait to share a marriage bed until after we get to know each other better and maybe even learn to like each other."

"I like you already, Thatcher. And I'm sorry you don't like me yet. I'll try harder—"

"No." The word came out almost harshly. He combed his fingers through his hair faster. "I like you too. But I want to wait until we *like*-like each other."

"What is *like-like?*"

He was botching this whole conversation badly. Maybe he'd known he would and that's why he'd avoided it. But he had to at least try to make her understand. "Since we didn't have the chance to court properly, I thought we could take some time to develop our affection for each other before we—well, before we share the marriage bed."

"Oh." The breathless word was filled with surprise.

He looked at her again, and that was a mistake, because she was now standing beside the bed, revealing the full length of the nightgown, which was a silky material that caressed her body and seemed to beckon him to do the same.

Swallowing hard, he forced his gaze to her face, but not before he saw the curve of her abdomen where the baby was definitely growing. She'd hidden it well beneath her garments.

"I don't want the marriage bed to be about *duty* or *marital rights*." He stumbled over the words, glad for the darkness to hide his embarrassment. "I want us to both *want* to be together."

She cocked her head. "I don't understand."

"We can develop affection for each other."

"I already told you that I like you. You're a kind and decent man."

"I want more than toleration of each other."

She seemed to be studying him. Then she sighed. "I'm sorry, Thatcher. Since I already do respect you, I don't know what you mean."

Had she never felt the sparks of attraction, the heat from a kiss, or the passion that could simmer between a man and a woman?

He'd assumed, since she'd been married, that she had some experience in those things. But what if the marriage bed with Charles had been nothing more than the *duty* and *marital rights* she'd referenced?

Thatcher's gut tightened at just the thought of Charles using Amelia so callously. From everything she'd revealed about her former husband, that was probably what had happened.

With her mother having left at such a young age, maybe Amelia had never seen what a loving and happy relationship should look like. Maybe she didn't know that a marriage could be filled with desire and affection.

His own mother and father had set a good example for him and his siblings. The two had been affectionate with each other. Not in a showy way, but in tender exchanges, sweet touches, and soft kisses.

Maybe it was his turn to provide an example and show Amelia what a true marriage could be like. He could teach her that a relationship consisted of more than what she'd had with Charles.

Of course, Thatcher wasn't an expert at relationships and had a lot yet to learn. But he'd experienced passion to a degree with Nora. She'd enjoyed kissing him, which they'd done more of after they were engaged. He'd also had some dalliances during his college years, enough to know that women didn't have to be passive participants and could enjoy intimacy every bit as much as a man.

"I'll try, Thatcher," she said again, softly. "That's what I was trying to show you tonight."

"You don't have to try." He spoke just as softly. "Let's just give our marriage some time and let our affection develop."

She hesitated. "I'm not sure how to let it develop."

"You don't have to do anything. I'll show you some ways." The moment the words were out of his mouth, heat crawled up his neck. What was he saying? He was being too brazen, wasn't he?

"Okay." This time her reply held a note of shyness.

"Besides," he said quickly, to alleviate the awkwardness,

"as we get to know each other better and like each other, affection will develop naturally." At least, he hoped it would.

She still had creases in her pretty forehead, but she nodded.

"Then we're in agreement that we'll put off the, uh, marriage bed until we're both ready."

"How will we know when that is?"

"I don't know. Hopefully we'll both just feel it."

She hugged her arms together and shivered.

He started toward the bed to gather up the covers, but as he stepped on a blanket on the floor, he swiped that up instead.

"Here." He stopped in front of her and draped it around her shoulders. He got a tiny glimpse of her cleavage before shielding her beautiful body behind the blanket.

How could he show her in this moment that he was attracted to her but in a way that wasn't lustful?

A part of him wanted to just walk out of the room and get away from the fire and temptation she presented. But if he wanted to demonstrate the kind of consensual physical attraction that was possible between a man and a woman, then he had to start sometime. Why not now?

He lifted his hand to her hair and drew a strand behind her ear, slowly and tenderly. He skimmed his fingers along her cheek until he reached her dimple. Then he bent down and gently kissed the spot.

She drew in a breath but didn't move.

"I've been wanting to do that since the evening I first laid eyes on you."

"You have?"

He traced the adorable indentation with his finger.

She breathed in again, and this time it was more pronounced.

He was doing it. He was causing her to feel something. Maybe getting his wife to fall in love with him and desire him as a man would be more fun than he'd realized.

He would work on winning her slowly but persistently. That would be his goal over the next weeks as they started their new life together.

In the meantime, they needed to have separate sleeping arrangements, mostly for his sake so that he could stay strong in his resolve.

He took a large step away from her. "I'll sleep up in the loft, and you can take the bed."

She clutched the blanket around her more tightly. "I don't want to disrupt you that way."

"It won't disrupt me." He backed into the doorway. "I want you to have the bed—you and the baby."

She opened her mouth as if she might argue with him. But how could she when it came to the baby? As if realizing the same, she closed her mouth, and her shoulders seemed to relax. "Thank you, Thatcher."

He wanted her to feel comfortable with him, wanted her to like being around him. But after all she'd gone through in her first marriage, it would take some time. Thankfully, he was a patient man.

"Good night, Amelia." With that, he exited the room and didn't look back.

"She's made great strides this week, thanks to you."

Thatcher's words of praise warmed Amelia as she stood at the entrance of the stall and watched him finish wrapping gauze around Queen's hoof.

"She's still got a ways to go before she heals." On one knee in the hay, Thatcher bent his head as he focused on Queen. "But eventually she'll be able to walk normally again."

He'd discarded his hat, and his fair hair lay flat, unlike in the morning when he'd just woken up and they ate breakfast together, which had quickly become one of her favorite times of the day—a time when they could relax over their meal, sip coffee, and talk about the families and animals he needed to visit.

Unruly hair or not, he was a handsome man, and he seemed to grow more so every day. Or maybe she was just noticing more things about him—like how he had a throbbing vein in his neck whenever he strained to do something, or how he had long fingers that held strength but also tenderness. He had a tiny scar on the back of one hand and a strand of hair that always fell over his forehead. His eyes changed shades of blue depending on his mood, and his jaw ticked when he was thinking hard about something.

Yes, she'd learned a lot about him during their first week of marriage. In fact, she knew more about her new husband after the short time of being with him than she'd known about Charles after two months.

One thing was certain . . . Thatcher Hoyt was a good man.

As though sensing her attention, he peeked up at her. "What are you thinking, sweetheart?"

He'd taken to calling her sweetheart, which she liked much more than she should, the same way she liked looking at him more than she should.

She dropped her attention to the leftover gauze she was wrapping back onto the roll. She couldn't very well tell him she'd been admiring him, so she said the next thing on her mind. "You're the one to thank for Queen's recovery, not me."

"We've been a team. But you've done more than I have."

Over the past six days since they'd brought Queen back to the farm, Amelia had spent countless hours soaking the horse's foot in cold water, cleaning it and rubbing it with ointment, and putting on fresh bandages. In fact, she'd spent more time in the barn than in the house, and still hadn't unpacked her bags. Thatcher had finally moved them into the bedroom, but Queen's care had taken priority over everything else.

In addition, she'd gone on all of Thatcher's calls with him except for the one he'd done in the middle of the night. He hadn't woken her and had been back before she'd risen at dawn.

Yesterday they'd gone to church, and there, Thatcher had introduced her to his cousin, his cousin's wife, and their three little children, who had invited them to come to their home for Christmas Day, which was only about a week away.

Thatcher had lingered after the service, enjoying talking to every person in the church, calling them by name and asking them about an animal or two that he'd helped them with. In return, everyone had greeted her warmly and welcomed her.

The way people treated her in this community versus Albany was starkly different, and she was relieved to have a husband who was well-liked instead of despised.

She loved the busyness of her life with Thatcher and that he had easily accepted her being his assistant not only at home with Queen but also on his calls. However, she was starting to feel guilty about the dishes and laundry piling up, the table growing even more cluttered, and the trail of muddy footprints that streaked the floor. Especially with Christmas so near.

She'd decided that today she would take some time to care for the house. Even though Thatcher didn't seem to mind the mess, she didn't want him to be disappointed in her as a wife.

In fact, the longer she was with him, the more she wanted him to like her. Because the longer she was with him, the more *she* liked *him*.

He was just so likable.

Maybe it also had to do with how kind he was to her. He went out of his way to help her the way a fine gentleman would a lady—with dismounting from the horse they were still borrowing from Mr. Oakley, opening doors for her, tucking her arm into his elbow when they walked, making sure she was always warm and comfortable, and so many other small kindnesses.

Not to mention how respectful he'd been of her regarding marital relations. He'd taken her by surprise when he'd told her he wanted to put off sharing the marriage bed until they had a chance to get to know each other and let affection develop between them. She'd been skeptical about his intentions, but after he'd slept in the loft the past week, she admired him for honoring his word.

At times, she worried he would change his mind

about being married to her. Maybe he would find something about her that he didn't like and cast her aside, especially since they hadn't consummated their union and he could still ask for an annulment.

On the other hand, he seemed happy with the way things were going, and he never complained that she was doing anything wrong. That had to be a good sign, didn't it?

He wrapped the last of the bandage around the mare's hoof, then stood and brushed the hay from his trousers. "That should get you through the morning," he said to Queen as he rubbed his long fingers over her silky black muzzle.

The horse nickered her response, probably liking Thatcher as much as everyone else.

Amelia hesitated only another moment before stepping back. "I suppose I had better go inside."

"You sure you don't want to ride into town with me?" Thatcher stooped to gather the supplies.

She did want to go with him, but then the house would remain untidy and unclean for another day. "You go on. I really need to do a few chores."

"Okay."

Did his voice sound disappointed? Maybe she ought to go after all. But no, she had to prove she was of some value to him as a wife, that she could manage a home and do all the things a wife was supposed to do.

He paused in his packing away the supplies. "Is there anything you need or that you'd like me to get you?"

There he was again, being so kind to her. At times like this, she wasn't sure how she'd picked so fine a candidate for her husband. She was fairly certain he was the best man out there and that no one else could begin to compare with him. All the more reason to do whatever she could to keep him.

Thatcher's warm blue eyes captured her and kept her from scampering away. "What are you craving today, sweetheart?"

Earlier in the week, she'd had a strange craving for mashed potatoes. She hadn't cared about the meat, had only wanted the potatoes. So when Thatcher had come into the house after taking care of the animals and seated himself at the table to a pan of mashed potatoes and nothing else, she'd admitted to having food cravings once in a while.

"I'm fine today. But thank you for asking."

"You're sure? Because I can stop and get you anything you want."

Should she admit that she'd been thinking about homemade noodles in butter sauce? She hadn't eaten homemade noodles in years, had only tasted them a time or two at community gatherings. So why was she craving them?

Thatcher's eyes twinkled. "I can tell you want something."

"How?"

"Because you hesitated." He gave Queen a final pat before stepping out of the stall and into the aisle beside Amelia. "And because you have a cute little wrinkle right here." He gently caressed her forehead where she'd apparently furrowed her brow.

At the contact, like most of the time, her senses homed in on his fingers, his closeness, his warmth. She was embarrassed to admit she was beginning to crave his touch more than any food.

He'd been touching her just briefly in passing all week—a squeeze of her hand, a stroke against her cheek, the tuck of hair behind her ear, or a caress to her shoulder. He'd been respectful with every contact, never lingering, never crossing a line, and never making her feel uncomfortable.

In fact, his touches had stirred a strange longing for more—more like the kiss he'd given her on her dimple that night in the bedroom. She wouldn't mind if he leaned in and kissed her cheek like that again.

But she didn't voice her opinion on the matter. He'd said she didn't need to do anything, that he'd be the one to lead. She wouldn't know what to do anyway.

With the bright morning sunlight streaming through the open barn door, his face was fully visible and his smile just waiting to be unleashed. Could she be the one to set it free this morning? If so, how?

"So what can I get my beautiful pregnant wife today?" His voice was light but contained a note of sincerity.

He was so sweet to her with the compliments too. He wasn't gushing over her or using flattery to gain favors from her. No, every time he said something nice, it was clear that he meant it.

She liked that he thought she was beautiful but that he complimented her about other things too—like her helpfulness, her company, her cooking, and more.

"Well?" He stuffed both hands into his pockets.

"I suppose you could purchase noodles."

His brows rose. "Noodles?"

"And maybe dill pickles?" She'd had a craving for those in the middle of last night when she'd had to get up and use the chamber pot. "I thought I'd cut up the pickles and mix them with buttered noodles for supper tonight."

He didn't respond, which meant she'd taken him by surprise again—at least, she hoped so.

"Doesn't that sound delicious?"

"I'm not sure . . ."

She fought back a smile. "I guarantee it will become your new favorite."

He studied her face for a moment, then his lips quirked.

"You'll love it."

"Is that so?" His smile crept out a little more.

She wanted to see it in all its breathtaking glory. "You'll like it even better if we sprinkle the pickle juice over it all."

And there it came. His lips curled up, revealing his straight teeth and bringing out more charm than any one man should ever be given.

At the sight of his grin, her heart leaped like a calf frolicking in the sunshine. She wanted to just stand and admire that happy, carefree smile of his. But she knew he needed to get going to town, and she needed to tend to the house.

As she made her way across the haymow and past the wagon, she could feel him watching her go. She paused at the barn door and shot a glance back at him. "You don't have to get anything for me, Thatcher. But if you do, I promise I won't make you eat the noodles and pickles together."

His chuckle was like more sunshine falling across her. She passed by the chickens, and as she crossed the snowy ground toward the cabin, contentment sifted through her.

To the west, the mountain ranges towered over the foothills and sprawling grassland where several families in the area owned ranches. To the east, on the opposite side of the barn, more mountain peaks touched the sky, all of them blanketed with thick snow. Although the cleared land around the cabin and barn was barren and the fields beyond were fallow, the lushness of the evergreens covered with snow made everything come to life.

She drew a breath of the cold air into her lungs and let a reverence settle over her. She would raise her family here and be a good mother to her children, unlike her own mother. Long ago she'd vowed that, if given the opportunity to have a child, she would be the opposite of her mother and never run off, never give up on a marriage, and never stop loving her child.

She wasn't sure what she'd done to disappoint her mother. What had been wrong with her that her mother hadn't been able to love her enough to stay? Hadn't even loved her enough to be a part of her life in some small way.

As she reached the stoop of the cabin, she paused and breathed in the crispness of the high-altitude air that contained a smoky, wood-burning scent. She placed a hand on the swell of her baby. "I will love you better, baby. I promise."

Once inside the cabin, she began heating water to wash dishes. She'd just rolled up her sleeves and started scrubbing when Thatcher stepped inside for a few seconds to let her know he was leaving and to say goodbye.

After he was gone, she tried not to think about how quiet the home was without him there and instead focused on the tasks that needed to be done. When the dishes were scrubbed and put away, she swept and washed the floor, picked up the sitting area, and then turned to survey the kitchen table with its heaps of stuff.

She needed to organize everything, but she wasn't a good organizer any more than Thatcher was.

Maybe she ought to also decorate a little for Christmas, but she'd never been a good decorator either. She hadn't done much at her childhood home, had always been too busy helping her father with the milking and other chores to bother with the house.

But a good wife would probably think about getting a Christmas tree or garland, trying to be festive in some way, maybe even by doing some special baking.

With her hands on her hips, she released an exasperated sigh. Standing and staring and wishing the mess would all magically go away wouldn't get her anywhere. But where should she start?

Tentatively she approached the table and picked up a newspaper. There were at least a dozen, if not more, of those. She could stack them neatly and perhaps place them in the basket next to the sofa, where someone had stored other newspapers and magazines.

She began placing the newspapers onto the bench, most of them out of Denver from the past months. As she did so, she made another pile of dirty towels and rags and odd socks. Then she gathered the mail into a bundle. Most of it seemed to be correspondence from Iowa addresses, perhaps from Thatcher's family or friends.

She lifted a newspaper to reveal several more

envelopes, each with a woman's name on the front. Eileen Smith. The address was New York City.

The name sounded vaguely familiar. Where had she heard it?

12

She fingered the top envelope and could feel a folded piece of paper inside.

Was Eileen Thatcher's ex-fiancée? He'd mentioned being engaged before moving to Colorado. But it hadn't seemed as though he'd wanted to discuss what had happened or why the wedding had been called off. Amelia hadn't pressured him, had sensed the topic was difficult for him and wanted to wait until he was ready to talk about it.

But with the distinctively feminine slant of the cursive writing on the envelope, a sense of apprehension seeped through her. What if Thatcher had been corresponding with his fiancée over the past months because he still had feelings for her? Because he'd wanted to get back together?

If so, what had happened to finally put an end to his hopes with Eileen and seek out a mail-order bride instead?

Amelia glanced at the door. It was still firmly shut, and Thatcher wouldn't be back for a while. What harm could come from peeking inside at the letter and learning a little bit more about this Eileen?

Two more letters rested on the table from Eileen that she could see. Of course, there might be more buried under other stuff. But she didn't have to read any of the others. She'd only take a quick look at this one—just to see who Eileen was and reassure herself the woman was no longer a part of Thatcher's life.

Amelia gingerly lifted the envelope flap and slipped the sheet out. As she unfolded it, she glanced in the direction of the door again. She really didn't want Thatcher catching her going through his mail. She knew it was wrong and that she wasn't respecting his privacy. But now that she'd discovered this woman's name among his correspondences, she needed to know what had happened.

The letter started out with a few niceties, the woman talking about her position as a domestic for a wealthy household and how she planned to put in her notice of termination soon.

"Thank you for your advice on traversing the mountain roads. I will do my best to arrive in Breckenridge this autumn since the winter is indeed lonely and long. I look forward to meeting you and hope that I will not disappoint you in any way."

Amelia halted and flattened her hand against her suddenly racing heart. Eileen. From New York City. Coming to marry Thatcher.

What was the name Thatcher had used at the wedding that night at the hotel? Had it been Eileen?

Amelia replayed the ceremony when they'd begun stating their vows. Yes, as a matter of fact, that's what it had been. He'd called her Eileen.

Amelia had assumed he'd used the name because of the confusion with her letters or because her envelopes had been smudged or because he'd forgotten her name.

But no, he'd called her Eileen because that was the name of his mail-order bride—a bride who had yet to arrive in Breckenridge and who would still be expecting to marry Thatcher and start a new life with him.

What would Thatcher do when he realized he'd married the wrong bride? He'd invited Eileen, asked her to marry him, and promised to provide for her. He wouldn't send her back, would he? Thatcher was too honorable to cast Eileen aside or ignore her. He would feel responsible for her. Maybe he would still want to marry her. After all, he'd exchanged letters with her and liked her enough that he'd asked her to be his bride. Eileen probably wouldn't have such a difficult past, wouldn't have to force herself to clean the house, and wouldn't prefer to accompany him on his visits.

Eileen was probably the perfect companion for Thatcher.

Amelia's legs began to tremble. She grabbed onto the edge of the table and lowered herself to a spot on the bench. Her hand shook with the letter, and she quickly tossed it down on the table as if somehow she could make it go away.

No wonder Thatcher had been confused about her being a widow and other details that hadn't seemed to match up. He'd been confused because she wasn't his bride. He wasn't the man in Breckenridge who she'd been communicating with.

If he wasn't the man, then who was the fellow she'd written to? Of course, she'd said in her letters that she wouldn't arrive until the spring, so wherever he was, he probably wouldn't expect her until then. When he discovered she'd arrived early and married another man, what would he think? Would he be upset?

Honestly, that was the least of her worries at the moment. The biggest issue was that Eileen was still in the picture. Although it was winter and traveling into the high country was difficult, there was still the possibility that Eileen could come any day. She might even be in the high country already and simply be stranded like Amelia had been.

What would happen if Eileen showed up? Could they convince her to marry another eager man? There were plenty around. But what if she insisted on marrying Thatcher? It would be within her right to do so.

"Oh my." Amelia bowed her head, feeling suddenly nauseous. How was she going to break this news to Thatcher? She had to tell him, didn't she? She couldn't go on and pretend that she hadn't discovered the mix-up. Thatcher needed to know the truth, that he'd gotten the wrong bride. He needed the freedom to marry Eileen, who probably wasn't a widow pregnant with a murdered man's child.

Amelia slipped the letter back into the envelope and placed it on top of the other two. If only she hadn't lost her bundle of letters, this wouldn't have happened. She would have married the right man—the man who was expecting her. Was it someone she'd met over the past week?

She sifted back through the faces of the various single men she'd met on visits with Thatcher or at church. She didn't remember names, but she honestly couldn't claim that she would want to marry any of them. None of them appealed to her. Even the men in her letters weren't appealing to her anymore.

The truth was, she didn't want anyone else . . . except Thatcher. After spending hours and hours with him over the past week and getting to know the truly amazing man that he was, she knew she'd never find another husband who was like him. He was a man of solid principle and character. He treated her with more respect and gentleness than anyone ever had before. And he'd made it clear he wanted a marriage that had more to it than just an exchange of duties.

She was beginning to see that a marriage could be built with friendship, companionship, and even working together. She hadn't felt any dread over the past week, not even that night she'd gone to his bed, because he treated her as an equal partner who deserved to be valued for who she was and not what she could give him.

How could she relinquish him and that kind of marriage?

She couldn't.

But how could she keep him when he wasn't really hers to begin with?

She couldn't.

Expelling a soft groan, she laid her forehead on the table. Everything inside her resisted the prospect of telling Thatcher anything about the mix-up, but she knew she would have to sooner rather than later.

Even though her mind was scattered with the new revelation, she managed to finish tidying the house, do the laundry, and make a batch of biscuits. As she stepped into the bedroom, she halted, put her hands on her hips, and stared at her bags. A part of her wanted to unpack them, as if in doing so she could claim her place there in the cabin. But did she really have that right?

She lowered herself to the edge of the bed, then expelled a long sigh. She should have known her relationship with Thatcher was too good to be true.

She twisted her wedding band. Even though it was simple and didn't have any embellishments or jewels, she loved it more with every passing day because it showed Thatcher's generosity and kindness. He hadn't known her, but he'd come to the wedding prepared to give her the ring.

Charles hadn't given her a ring, not even after they were married. In fact, she couldn't remember ever having any jewelry. Her mother hadn't left any of hers behind, and her father had never been able to afford any.

She fingered the ring. Would she have to give it back since Thatcher had meant it for a different woman?

At the distant clopping of horse hooves, she stood. With the afternoon turning into evening, Thatcher was probably returning from town.

Her stomach churned with sudden nausea. For once, she wasn't eager to see him and wanted to put it off. He'd probably take one look at her face and realize something was wrong.

What should she do about Eileen's letters?

She jumped up and raced into the other room. The envelopes were spread out over the table right where she'd left them.

With a racing heart, she swiped them up and glanced

around the room. She wasn't really considering hiding the letters, was she?

Her gaze locked in on the basket of newspapers. She quickly crossed to it, knelt beside it, then lifted half the newspapers. She slipped the three letters into the stack, set them back down, and then stood.

She ignored the guilt starting to poke at her. She would only hide them until she figured out what she was going to say to Thatcher.

The best thing was just to tell him right away.

Yes, that's what she would do.

As his horse pattered to a halt in front of the cabin, she straightened her shoulders and started toward the door. With each step, her heart pounded with dread, and by the time she reached the door, she felt like she was going to a funeral.

She placed her hand on the door, but it swung open before she could do anything, and there stood Thatcher, his smile as wide as the mountain sky overhead, and his eyes filled with excitement. "I have a Christmas present for you."

He was holding one hand behind his body, concealing something from her.

"A Christmas present?" She took a step back.

"Yes." He brought his hand around and held out a wool coat in a pretty blue. It was trimmed with black velvet, and the lining inside looked warm and thick.

"Oh, Thatcher." She stroked it but then pulled her hand back. "It's too nice. I couldn't accept it."

His smile only stretched wider. "You need it, especially since you'll be going with me on so many calls."

She fingered the velvet trim this time. "Thatcher, you shouldn't have."

"I wanted to." His voice gentled. "Besides, like I said, it's a Christmas present."

"But I can't get you anything." She hadn't even thought about getting him a present. She had only pennies left, and what would that buy?

"I have everything I want right here." He swept his gaze over her, leaving a warm trail in its wake.

She could feel a flush moving into her cheeks. "Seriously, Thatcher."

"I am serious. You needed the new coat, and the General Store had this one. I had to get it for you."

She finally took it from him and hugged it against her chest. "Thank you."

"And please, don't feel like you have to reciprocate. Okay?"

"I want to do something for you for Christmas."

"Then go with me to cut down a tree and help me decorate it. Maybe tomorrow?"

That wasn't the same as giving him a gift.

"Please?" he pleaded in a sweet voice before she could say so.

What about those letters from Eileen? She hesitated. Now wasn't the right time to say anything about them. Not when he was doing something so nice for her. Not with him watching her and waiting so expectantly.

"Okay." She couldn't keep from smiling back at him. His happiness was always contagious.

Tomorrow. She would bring up Eileen's letters tomorrow. For tonight, though, she would just put them from her mind and pretend everything was all right.

13

Amelia exited the barn and swallowed the reservations that had been lodging in her throat since yesterday, when she'd found Eileen's letters. She blinked against the bright morning sunshine, her eyesight quickly adjusting after the dim lighting of the barn, where she'd spent the past hour tending to Queen's hoof.

Thatcher stood by the well, hoisting up a bucket of water, probably to fill the troughs. His coat strained against his arms and shoulders as he hefted the rope and the heavy load. Wearing his gloves and tall boots and a Stetson over his unruly hair, he made a fine, fine picture—as rough and rugged as the craggy boulders that rose in the foothills behind him.

Her heart pinched sharply. Would she lose him today?

No. She had to find a way to keep him, keep what they had, keep him from giving her up once he learned she wasn't the bride he'd sent away for.

Could she refrain from informing him until after they went to cut down the Christmas tree later today? Or maybe she should wait until after Christmas. After all, she didn't want to ruin the day.

They'd had an enjoyable evening last night eating the noodles coated with butter and cheese, and with pickles on the side. They'd teased and talked all through the meal. Afterward, she'd helped him restock his medical bag with the fresh supplies he'd brought home. Then, as they'd taken their usual spots in front of the fireplace—he in the chair and she on the sofa—he'd read aloud from the latest newspaper he'd purchased with the tales of White River War.

Amelia didn't know much about the natives who lived in Colorado, had only heard of the conflict that had happened back in September when Utes in eastern Colorado had attacked an agent on their reservation, killing him and his employees while taking their women and children as captives.

The newspaper article told about another attack, this one against US troops just north of the reservation, in which a major and thirteen men had also been killed.

Amelia had heard tales of the conflict between the natives and the new settlers from time to time while she'd been growing up. But it had all seemed so far away and foreign.

Now that she was here in the middle of the West that had once belonged to the natives, she supposed she could understand why the natives were fighting to keep their land. It was wild and untamed and untouched by the industries that filled the East with massive cities that were busy and crowded to capacity.

Charles had predicted that the local farms around Albany would one day give way to more industries. He'd claimed the change was inevitable, which he'd used as justification for taking the land away from the farmers who'd been there for generations and selling it to the highest bidders.

Was the same thing happening in the West with the natives? The land being taken for the sake of progress?

Whatever the case, Amelia was sad to hear about the conflict with the natives. She and Thatcher had discussed the issue, both of them wishing there was a way to resolve it more peacefully. Their conversation had been deep and thoughtful and interesting.

Maybe if they had more such good evenings, they would draw closer so that he got the affectionate relationship he'd said he wanted.

She held out her hand and examined her wedding band. Thatcher had said, *"To my way of seeing things, we're married and made a binding commitment that I'm not planning to end because of any hardships we face."* He was an honorable man, and she knew he meant what he said.

The trouble was, he hadn't realized he'd married the wrong woman when he'd said it.

What if she didn't tell him about the mail-order-bride mistake until Eileen actually showed up? That might not be until spring now, and that would allow plenty of time for their relationship to develop. Could she even work on winning him so that he would fall in love with her?

Love had never been a part of her husband requirements before. Love hadn't been a part of any of her marriage plans. She was too realistic to allow herself any hope that she would experience love.

But if love would keep Thatcher interested in her instead of Eileen, then she had to consider it. And yet, how could she keep such a secret for months? She'd feel like she was living a lie.

She began to cross toward him, her boots sinking in the wet layer of snow that had fallen over the night.

She knew the second he caught sight of her, because he paused briefly to watch her approach before resuming his winding of the rope.

"The coat suits you," he called.

She brushed a hand over the thick, warm wool. "I've been much warmer this morning."

"Good." He cocked his head toward the barn. "How is Her Royal Majesty?"

"She's not as restless and seems more content."

"Well, that's good. We wouldn't want to upset Her Queenship."

Amelia's lips twitched with the need to smile. Thatcher had that effect upon her.

He hefted the bucket up the rest of the way, then guided it toward the stone edge of the well and rested it there.

She wasn't sure why she was approaching him, except that she somehow wanted to start winning him and making him fall in love with her . . . before Eileen showed up. How did a woman go about earning a man's love?

She wasn't well-versed in such matters. All she knew was that she had to try so that she didn't lose him.

As she reached the well, she latched on to one side of the bucket handle, intending to help him carry it back to the barn.

He didn't protest her hold, but as he hefted the bucket between them, she could feel him take most of the weight.

Slowly, so that they didn't slosh the water out, they started back to the barn. "Do you think she'll ever be well enough for someone to ride her?"

"She might always have a limp, but I imagine she'll be able to handle you."

Amelia bit back a frustrated sigh. She just hoped she was still around when Queen was better and able to ride. But she had no guarantees.

"Look." Thatcher halted and pointed ahead to the woodland of evergreens that bordered the strawberry field.

Amelia paused, her breath coming out in puffs of white in the cold morning air, even with the sunshine bathing her head. She looked in the direction Thatcher was pointing to find a herd of what appeared to be oversized deer grazing in the tall grass that hadn't yet been flattened by snow.

There had to be thirty or more quietly eating, their ears flicking with attentiveness. Some had antlers and others none. But all were the same dull brown. Their heads had a thick build, similar to cattle, but their tales were short and stubby like those of deer.

"Deer?" she asked softly.

"Elk." Thatcher lowered the bucket of water to the ground without taking his gaze off the herd. "Called wapiti by the Shawnee."

"Wapiti." She rolled the unfamiliar word over her tongue.

"I've been told the elk herds can get quite large in the winter." Thatcher spoke reverently, his eyes on the herd. "In the spring and summer, they break up into smaller bands as they have calves and find fresh grasslands."

"The antlers on some of them are so big." And majestic, reaching backward half the length of the elk's body in some cases.

"Apparently the males grow new antlers every year. I visited a man over the summer who shot a bull and had the antlers on his wall. He said they weighed a good thirty pounds."

"I can't imagine how the bull carries that kind of weight around on his head."

"They must have muscular necks."

One of the males turned toward them, as if realizing he had an audience. The creatures were too far away to worry about a stampede or an attack. Even so, she sidled closer to Thatcher.

At the brush of her arm, he shifted his hand so that his fingers grazed her back. She could hardly feel the touch through her coat, but she liked that he welcomed her so openly and was so gentle in return.

Was this an opportunity to do more to make him happier with their relationship? But what should she do?

He'd reached out to her in little ways every day with small touches and caresses, like the one on her back. Maybe she could do the same to him.

She took a step even nearer and rested her head against him. In the next instant, his hand at her back circled her waist. All the while, he continued to watch the herd, his expression unchanging, his eyes wide with admiration.

She hesitated only a moment, then slipped her arm around his back too, so they were standing side by side. It seemed natural enough for her to do so, and thankfully, he didn't react or say anything.

Neither of them spoke as they took their fill of one of the most beautiful sights in all of creation, with the herd grazing peacefully in the snowy grassland against the backdrop of the craggy hills and mountains.

She loved being in the crook of his body, having his strength holding her up, being there to support him and receive his support. It was a new and unfamiliar feeling but not unwanted.

She burrowed into his side, a strange warmth rushing through her that made her want to be closer and feel more of him. The hard length of his abdomen, the tautness of his arm, the possessive clasp of his hand—she was attuned to it all . . . and a part of her wanted to go on standing there like that all day.

But she couldn't. She had to say or do something. "It's beautiful, Thatcher."

"It is." His voice was low. "I'm glad I get to see this with you."

"I'm glad I get to see it with you too."

She felt him shift. In the next instant, he pressed a kiss against her hair on top of her head. It was somewhat hard and lingering. And his arm behind her tightened.

He'd kissed her on their wedding night and then her dimple once. But he hadn't kissed her again until this moment. She liked it. A lot. And she had no desire to pull away. In fact, she had a sudden urge to kiss him back. It didn't have to be a long kiss. She'd make sure it was short.

Before she lost her nerve, she tilted her head up. Then quickly and decisively, she lifted onto her toes and touched her mouth to his. She didn't know a lot about kissing, had never initiated one with Charles, had always felt as though she was enduring his unwanted attention. But this time, she needed to communicate something to Thatcher—perhaps that she was willing, that she wanted more, that she would do whatever he wanted so that she could keep him.

For a few seconds, he didn't seem to respond and held himself motionless.

Was he merely surprised by her boldness? Or was he repulsed by it and wishing she'd kept to herself?

Mortification began to sift through her. Finding the letters yesterday and fearing losing Thatcher was foremost on her mind. But that didn't mean she had to make a fool of herself.

She started to back up, removing her mouth from his. But before she made it more than an inch, he dove in and captured her lips with his, not letting her get away. His mouth was warm, almost deliciously so. And the pressure was firm and full but not overpowering.

He meshed his lips with hers in a motion that seemed to urge her to mesh hers back, to move against him in a sort of dance that was slow and tender and sweet. It was a new dance—one she'd never learned or done before. But Thatcher didn't hurry her, letting her catch up and allowing her to move at her own pace.

His arm was still around her, but somehow hers had dropped from his back, and now she lifted both hands to his chest where his coat was open. She pressed her palms to his shirt, relishing the broad hardness beneath her hands.

His other arm encircled her so that she was standing in his embrace, one strong arm on either side of her. Surrounded by him on all sides, she felt entirely safe and cherished and somehow knew he would never hurt her, that he would protect her more than he would protect himself.

The realization brought a swell of emotion into her chest. She didn't understand it, but she did know that she wanted to be closer to him, that she wanted to press her mouth forcefully to his, as if that could somehow satisfy a need for him that was building low inside.

She mingled her mouth against his more urgently, the need driving her.

As though she'd just given him permission to set free something inside himself, he responded by tangling his lips with hers more deeply and thoroughly. Although the tenderness was still there—along with the delectable feeling of being cherished—his mouth moved with a passion and power that hadn't been there before.

His kiss seemed to sweep her off her feet so that she was floating, weightless, clinging to him to keep from flying away altogether with a keen pleasure that swirled through her in increasing intensity.

She'd never experienced anything like it before, not even close. And she could only rise into him and kiss him harder, hoping her kiss was communicating everything she was feeling and just how much she loved the connection of their mouths and bodies.

Was this what he'd been hinting at when he'd said he wanted more than just duty and rights for their marriage bed? Was there a mutual passion that could be part of it? A passion that she hadn't experienced yet but that could still be hers with Thatcher?

If he still wanted her when he found out about his real bride . . .

Eileen. She couldn't forget about Eileen.

Amelia released her hold of Thatcher, pulled back, and spun away.

Her lungs were heaving. Her heart was racing. And her entire body felt like it was on fire—in a way that was a form of exquisite torture.

A part of her wanted to turn back around, fling herself into his arms, then kiss him again and this time never stop. But she had to stop. She had to keep their physical relationship from progressing too far until she had the chance to explain to him the mistake they'd made.

"I'm sorry, Amelia." His voice was breathless, almost hoarse.

Just the sound of it sent a strange current of need skating along her nerves.

"I got a little carried away," he continued. "I didn't mean for the kiss to get so . . . so . . ."

"It's all right, Thatcher." Her voice was breathless too, and she lifted her hands to her hot cheeks.

"I should have used more restraint."

She shook her head, then drew in a deep breath and readied herself. She had to say the words before she found another excuse.

"Mr. Hoyt!" Pounding horse hooves accompanied the shout from the front lane that led to the cabin. "Mr. Hoyt!"

Someone needed Thatcher's veterinarian services. Amelia was beginning to understand what the visits and the calls meant. And from the urgency in this newcomer's voice, she guessed the need was probably an emergency.

Thatcher began to stride down the lane in the direction of the visitor—a young man in cowboy gear who was obviously hired help at one of the nearby ranches. Rusty, who'd been sitting by the barn, rose and limped toward the horse and rider, barking a loud welcome.

Amelia didn't quite know what to do, was still too flustered by the kiss with Thatcher to think clearly. So she stood unmoving next to the bucket of well water.

As the rider curved the bend that led to the barn, he reined in sharply, his worried eyes finding Thatcher. "Mr. Hoyt, glad you're here. Beckett's horse has colic and is in real bad pain and ain't doing well. Sterling sent me to fetch you and see if you could come right away."

Thatcher gave a curt nod. "Tell him I'll be there just as soon as I can."

"He doesn't want the horse suffering any longer than it has to."

"Neither do I." Thatcher's brow furrowed with concern. "I'll saddle my horse and be right over."

The ranch hand gathered up his reins. "Much obliged."

Thatcher was already striding to the barn. He tossed Amelia a glance. "I'll saddle your horse if you grab my bag."

"I will." She scurried toward the cabin, a surge of pleasure pouring through her. He hadn't even questioned her coming along with him. He'd assumed she would and had included her. And she loved that, loved being a part of his work and his life.

Now she just had to find a way to *stay* a part of his work and life . . .

14

"How long has the horse been in pain?" Thatcher halted against the corral fence just outside the horse barn.

The roan gelding was staggering around inside, butting the split rails, frantic to escape. The poor creature didn't realize that he wouldn't be able to get away from the pain by running off somewhere else, that the pain was inside him.

Sterling Noble stood at the corral fence already, his face shadowed beneath the brim of his hat. "Noticed him acting strange last night." The man in charge of the sprawling Noble Ranch, Sterling was intense and serious, and tension radiated from his weathered features and strong shoulders.

Beckett, the Noble Ranch foreman, paced inside the corral, holding a head collar. "Thought he was suffering from constipation, so I gave him a dose of black draught, but that only seemed to make him more agitated."

The black draught could help with the colic, constipation, or a belly ache if one of those was the problem. But from a quick assessment of the gelding, Thatcher suspected something more was wrong.

The snorting roan stumbled but then righted himself, his head lolling back and forth. He was gnashing his teeth and foaming at the mouth. His nostrils were dilated, and his eyes contained wildness and confusion.

Thatcher nodded at the horse collar. "Let's get the collar on so I can examine him."

Amelia was beside him at the corral, her pretty eyes crinkled with worry as she watched the gelding. Even so, the morning sunshine made the gold flecks in her hazel eyes sparkle, bringing back the image of her eyes when she'd kissed him a little while ago—wide, nervous, and yet filled with longing.

She had kissed *him*.

His heart pattered with a few extra beats despite the gravity of the situation with the Nobles' gelding. The truth was, he hadn't been able to get the kiss out of his mind since the moment he'd stepped away from her in the barnyard. She had taken him by surprise not only in starting the kiss but also in staying there and seeming to relish every moment of it.

What a kiss it had been, filled with passion and longing and exploration, as if she'd never been kissed quite like that and was experiencing a truly moving kiss for the first time.

It had moved him. In fact, it had bucked him off his saddle and landed him on his backside on the ground with the wind knocked out of him. He wasn't sure exactly why he'd reacted so strongly to the kiss, and he hadn't had much time to think about it in light of the urgent call to the Noble Ranch. But he suspected the reason the kiss had affected him was that Amelia affected him in a way no other woman had.

Even just standing there beside her as the concern radiated from her beautiful face, how could he not be affected?

A swell of emotion rose swiftly inside his chest. He hadn't known her long, but was he already falling in love with her? Had it been love at first sight, the same way it had been for the previous couple who had lived on his farm? Maybe there was something in the air there that heightened the love and made it blossom more quickly.

Or maybe it was just that she was the perfect woman for him, and he had Providence to thank for bringing them together.

Whatever the case, the past week had been one of the best of his life. He'd enjoyed every moment with her, whether working alongside her or sitting with her in the evenings. He couldn't deny he was falling for her fast.

Now with that kiss between them, what would happen next? He didn't want to rush things, but how long did he have to wait before he could kiss her again?

Beckett was approaching the gelding slowly and carefully. He was a lanky fellow but was quick and strong, like most cowboys. He was less serious than Sterling, had a ready smile and a sharp wit.

The foreman had sent away for a mail-order bride too. He hadn't talked much about it, certainly not as much as Thatcher had. But of course, that probably had to do with the fact that Beckett's bride wasn't coming until the spring, after the snow thaw. Thatcher just hoped Beckett's bride turned out to be as good as his—although he wasn't sure how that was possible.

From the sound of things, Sterling seemed to be happy with his own new bride. He'd just gotten married a couple of weeks ago to Violet, the love of his life. Because of some danger that Violet and her sister Hyacinth had been in, Beckett had temporarily pretended to be engaged to Hyacinth for her protection.

Of course, the engagement wasn't real—never had been and never would be, especially because the two fought like a cat and dog. However, the community still had the notion that Beckett and Hyacinth were together and planning to get married. It didn't help that Beckett persisted in pretending in order to bother Hyacinth. But that was Beckett.

As the foreman closed in on his gelding, he worked with a confidence that came from years of experience.

Before the gelding could get away, Beckett had the collar around him and was pulling him to a halt.

Thatcher began to make his way to the gate and could sense Amelia following behind. She'd proven herself to be indispensable during his calls, assisting him without so much as batting an eyelash at all the things she'd witnessed. He loved that about her, loved that she wanted to be there with him, loved that she cared enough to help.

Yes, he had to admit, he was falling in love with her. He'd always hoped to have a loving relationship with his mail-order bride, and he'd wanted to give them time for affection to grow. He'd just never imagined his feelings would develop so strongly and so quickly.

For a short while, he forced himself to focus on the gelding. First, he did his usual external assessment. The horse's heart rate was too fast, the mucous membranes in the eyelids too red, and the temperature too high. Something more serious was definitely going on.

Thatcher washed up in a bucket of warm water that another ranch hand brought him, soaped up his arm, and then did a rectal examination. It didn't take him long to discover that the small intestine seemed to be in a knot and was cutting off the blood supply to the rest of the intestines. With the strangulation—the torsion—the horse would most certainly continue to suffer extreme pain.

Thatcher probed for a few more long moments before

slipping his arm out and submerging it into the bucket of water Amelia held out.

Sterling, Beckett, and several other ranch hands had gathered around the horse and were now watching him and waiting for his prognosis. He hated this part of his job, where he had to deliver bad news and disappoint people. But the truth was, he couldn't save every animal. It just wasn't possible. And in this case, it would be cruel to the horse to prolong his life.

While Thatcher scrubbed his arm in the soapy water, he finally met Beckett's gaze. "I'm sorry, but as far as I can tell, he has a torsion. His intestine is twisted up pretty badly."

Beckett didn't blink. "What can you do for him?"

"I've seen emergency surgeries performed for torsions." He'd participated in one such surgery in college. "But I don't have the equipment for a surgery of that magnitude, and even if I did, there's still a big chance it's too late."

"What about a shot of morphine?" This question came from Sterling.

"The morphine would only drag out his pain longer than necessary."

The horse gave a desolate whinny and lolled his head to one side.

Sterling brushed a hand down the horse's mane while Beckett murmured to the horse.

Thatcher gave his arms one last scrub, then took the towel Amelia offered. "I suggest we put him out of his misery as soon as possible."

Beckett was holding the collar and narrowed his eyes on Thatcher. "Just like that?" His Southern accent was strong today. "You're not gonna try anything at all?"

"Like I said, surgery would be a gamble."

Beckett spat out a piece of hay that he'd been chewing on. "What about going back in and trying to untangle the intestines."

"That's not how it works." Thatcher finished drying his arm and paused to face Beckett directly. "The intestine is already dying from lack of blood flow, and toxins are pumping into his blood."

"If you untangle the intestine, then everything will be all right."

"I can't manually untangle it. It's knotted too tightly."

"You can't give up." Beckett rubbed the horse's flank, which was sweaty. "You've got to try something."

"He's in agony—"

"I see that." Beckett's voice rose. "Which is why you need to figure out something."

"There is nothing else."

"Do. Something. Now." Beckett rose to his full height and took a menacing step toward Thatcher.

Thatcher held out a hand. "Whoa, now."

"What good are you as a veterinarian if you can't help when it's really needed?"

Sterling took a step to block Beckett from getting any nearer. He shot the foreman a warning glare before facing Thatcher. "This is Beckett's horse from forever. The one he rode when he came west. So it means a lot to him."

"I wish there was more I could do." Thatcher began to roll down his sleeve. "But there isn't a way to fix this."

A quiet settled around the corral. At the closing of a door at the main house across the yard, Thatcher guessed the womenfolk had come out to watch, likely having heard or seen Beckett's agitation.

Maybe it would be best for Amelia to go into the house and wait with them inside while the horse was shot. Putting an animal down, no matter how merciful, wasn't something the women needed to see.

"Sterling, would it be all right if Amelia went inside with your wife—"

"Amelia?" Beckett shoved Sterling aside and peered at Amelia.

Amelia stared back at Beckett, her face growing pale.

"I thought I was writing to Eileen." Thatcher had needed to explain the name mix-up to others over the past week, even though he still couldn't quite explain it to himself. "But it turns out her name is Amelia."

"My mail-order bride's name is Amelia." Beckett took a step forward, and this time Sterling didn't get in the way. "Amelia Stone, a widow from Albany, New York."

As he spoke now, something inside Thatcher shifted with a strange dread.

Beckett scanned Amelia from her head to her toes. "Five feet five inches, brown hair, hazel eyes, and dimples. That's the description in the advertisement and in the first letter I received from Amelia. Seems to match pretty well."

It did match perfectly. Even so, this Amelia didn't belong to Beckett. Thatcher drew her in closer. She was his. All his.

He cleared his throat. "Your Amelia isn't coming until the spring."

"Maybe she came early." Beckett held Amelia's gaze as though seeking the truth in her eyes.

Thatcher wanted to push Amelia behind him. Why had he brought her here to the Noble Ranch in the first place? He should have made her stay at home this time.

Even as the irrational considerations rushed through his head, one thought pushed to the front of his mind—Amelia wasn't denying anything.

Her eyes were wide, and she was still staring at Beckett.

"Tell him he's wrong, Amelia." Thatcher spoke to her gently. "Tell him you came here to marry me."

She swallowed hard, opened her mouth to say something, then closed it.

Everyone had grown silent, the poor horse's groans and grunts the only sounds in the morning air.

Thatcher had to put an end to this nonsense and take care of the suffering horse. He began to guide Amelia away from the horse and toward the corral gate. "Let's get you into the house—"

"I did come early." Her words tumbled out. "I wasn't supposed to come until spring."

Thatcher stopped abruptly and released her.

Amelia clasped her hands together, twisting her fingers. "It all happened so fast that night at the hotel. Everyone claimed Thatcher was the one waiting for me. And since I'd left my letters behind and didn't remember the name, I assumed they were right."

"No." Thatcher lifted his hat and combed his unruly waves before setting his hat back in place. "You're the woman I was waiting for. I'm certain of it."

Amelia's eyes filled with apology. "I found Eileen's letters yesterday when I was cleaning the cabin."

"Then you can confirm they're yours." He didn't care that his voice sounded pathetically desperate.

Amelia pressed her lips together, but her expression said everything.

He shook his head. This wasn't happening to him.

"I'm sorry, Thatcher. I was going to tell you today. I really was."

He shifted and gazed unseeingly at the mountain

peaks beyond the ranch. Amelia belonged to Beckett, was *his* mail-order bride, the one he'd been waiting for. Thatcher had no right to her, and in fact, his real bride was out there somewhere and still making her way to him, expecting him to marry her.

How had he made this big a mistake? He should have known from the moment he'd seen Amelia that she wasn't Eileen. None of the details and facts had matched up. Not even her name.

Had he just gotten so swept away in the need to have a wife that he'd allowed himself to ignore the warnings and his good judgment?

"Looks like you're taking what's mine, Thatcher." Beckett's hard comment was like an arrow into Thatcher's chest. It deflated him and took the life from him all at once. "You stole my bride, and now you're wanting to kill my horse."

Thatcher couldn't move and certainly didn't know how to respond to Beckett when both of his claims were true.

"What did I ever do to you to deserve your backstabbing?" Beckett's accusation rang out in the silence. "You're a poor excuse for a veterinarian and a poor excuse for a neighbor. I'll make sure everyone knows it."

"Hey now." Sterling's rebuke cut through the echo of Beckett's words. "You know Thatcher saved our cattle, and it sounds like this business with the bride was all an honest mistake."

"I doubt it." Beckett's bitter words only added to the despair rolling around inside Thatcher. "I want my bride. She's mine. Not yours."

Sterling began to cross to Thatcher. "Listen," he said gravely while darting a glance at Amelia, who'd hung her head and was obviously mortified by everything that had just happened. "Why don't you go on home and work this out."

"But the horse—"

"I'll take care of putting him down."

"I can try to do more." Thatcher didn't want anyone to think he'd given up, that he hadn't done his job and didn't deserve to be a veterinarian. He'd already run from such accusations once and had hoped he could do better this time. But apparently not.

Sterling waved a hand at the gate. "You've done all you can, Thatcher. Best to be on your way."

There wasn't anything encouraging about Sterling's words. The fellow probably was just as disappointed in him as Beckett was.

Thatcher expelled a taut breath and gave a curt nod. Then he touched Amelia's arm to lead her away.

She pulled back from him and, without a word or glance his way, strode to the gate.

"She's my mail-order bride, Thatcher," Beckett called.

"She belongs to me. You can't keep her. I'll expect you to figure out a way to get the marriage nullified just as soon as you can and then bring her to me."

Thatcher didn't know how to respond, so he kept silent. With his heart dropping hard to the bottom of his chest, he followed after Amelia. The situation felt familiar, as if he'd already lived this nightmare—the one where he lost his woman, his reputation, and the respect of those in the community.

The only thing different this time was that he wasn't just losing a fiancée. He was losing his wife, the woman he was married to, the woman he loved. Yes, he loved Amelia in a way he'd never loved anyone else.

But he had no right to have her. None. And he guessed she knew it too.

The ride back to the farm was silent.

Amelia was too ashamed to speak a word.

From the stiff way Thatcher held himself, it was easy to see he was upset and angry and hurt. He was probably also embarrassed by everything, maybe even humiliated that the news about their mistaken relationship and wedding had surfaced while they were out on a call.

If she'd just told him yesterday about finding Eileen's letters, or even this morning, she could have prevented the public disgrace of having him make all the ardent claims about her being his wife, especially in front of Beckett.

Now she knew who her real groom-to-be was and the one she'd been corresponding with in Breckenridge.

Beckett. The name was definitely familiar. He did work on a ranch with the livestock. And he'd been expecting her in the spring. All the facts made sense. No doubt if she asked him, he'd pull out the few letters she'd written and show them as proof of their communication.

As Amelia dismounted near the barn, her gaze caught on the bucket of water still in the middle of the yard where they'd left it. The elk were no longer grazing along the woodland. The beautiful moment of kissing Thatcher was over. And so was her marriage to him.

Because she couldn't stay married to Thatcher, could she? Not when Beckett was her intended, not when he was angry about the mix-up, and not when he was accusing Thatcher of stealing her.

Thatcher had dismounted too and was rubbing Rusty's head as the dog wagged his tail and begged for affection.

She hesitated near her horse. Should she go back to the cabin and pack her bags? Maybe she ought to go check on Queen one last time?

She reached for her horse's lead line.

"I'm sorry, Amelia." Thatcher scratched behind Rusty's ears, his broad shoulders slumping.

"You don't have anything to be sorry for. I'm the one who needs to apologize for not telling you when you got home yesterday that I found Eileen's letters."

"But things didn't match up." He kept his attention focused on the dog. "I knew it from the start, and I just ignored it."

"It's my fault for not bringing my letters and not

remembering names and not being more careful about clearing things up before our wedding."

"I could have questioned you more too."

Their wedding evening had moved quickly with so many people milling about and pressuring them. It would have been difficult to slow the momentum. "I guess I just wanted it to be true. I wanted to marry a man who was different from Charles, and from everything I heard about you and how much people liked and respected you . . ."

Thatcher's hand on Rusty stilled, and his head dropped so that his chin rested on his chest. "You should know that I've been keeping something from you too."

Something ominous in his tone told her she wouldn't like what he had to say.

Her pulse, which had been running at twice the speed since leaving the Noble Ranch, slowed to a crawl.

He straightened, drew in a breath, then seemed to force himself to look at her. "I'm not all that different from Charles. I had to leave Iowa because I ruined my practice and people no longer liked me or respected me."

She couldn't imagine people not liking or respecting Thatcher. He was so kind and generous and easy to talk to. "What happened?"

He shifted his gaze to the chickens that were strutting out of the barn. But he stood motionless, as though he'd traveled to another place and time.

She wanted to go to him and reassure him that no

matter what had happened in his past, he *was* different from Charles, that there was simply no comparison between them. But she knew she had to let Thatcher say his piece.

He hesitated. One of the hens pecked at the toe of his boot, but he didn't shoo it away. "It was back in April, at the start of the foaling season. Nora's family—"

"Nora was your fiancée?"

"Yes, she was someone I knew growing up. And after I returned to Cedar Rapids when I finished veterinarian school, we reconnected. We got engaged last December and were planning to get married in the summer."

Already, Amelia could tell that she wasn't going to like Nora.

"Her father breeds mares and has developed a big business selling quality foals for a high price." He paused as the same hen poked at his boot again. "The short of the story is that one of his best-bred foals got sick—probably sepsis. I stayed with the foal day and night, trying to save him. I didn't get enough sleep, let myself get exhausted, dozed off, and wasn't paying attention to a lantern that got knocked over."

She could picture Thatcher working tirelessly. She'd witnessed him doing it on their calls over the past week, going above and beyond for everyone every time.

"The fire was raging out of control and had engulfed a portion of the barn before I realized what had happened." His voice dropped with anguish. "I called for help and got some of the mares out. But over half of them—a dozen—were burned alive."

"It sounds like a mistake, Thatcher."

His expression was tight. "It doesn't matter. I should have seen the fire sooner, should have noticed the lantern wasn't hung the way it needed to be, should have realized the wind had gusted, should have noticed the sparks, should have at least smelled the smoke."

"Surely others could have seen it—"

"It was the middle of the night. No one else was there. I was the one responsible."

Something about his story didn't sound quite right—or complete. "I can't imagine, even with how exhausted you were, that you would leave a lantern unattended."

He stared at the hen still milling about his feet, now joined by another one that was clucking and scolding him.

"Who was negligent with the lantern, Thatcher?"

He sighed, then lifted his gaze. His blue eyes were murky with all the emotions that had been stirred in his soul. "Nora had come out to keep me company for a while, and she left the lantern by the back barn door when she snuck out."

"And she let you take the blame for the fire?"

"She wanted to tell her father she'd been there and that the fire was her fault. But I didn't want to hurt her reputation by having everyone know we'd been in the barn alone."

The dislike for Nora swelled. And something else hot mingled with it. Was it jealousy? "I take it the two of you were—you know."

"No, nothing like that," Thatcher rushed to say. "We may have been doing some kissing, but that's all."

Somehow, his words took away a little bit of the heat, the jealousy, although she didn't quite know why. "The fire wasn't your fault, Thatcher."

"I take full responsibility." His tone held a stubbornness that told her he wouldn't be swayed. "I shouldn't have let Nora come out and be with me. I knew we were sneaking around and that it wasn't right."

Amelia admired Thatcher for his willingness to sacrifice for Nora, but she disliked the woman even more.

"After the fire, Nora's family—her father—told me I was no longer welcome to practice in the community, that I was done and he'd make sure of it. I paid him what I could for his losses and the damages, sold off everything I had of value, and then I left."

"Nora could have told her father the truth privately."

"I didn't want her to."

"But she let you take the blame, and that's not right and that's not love. If she'd confessed to her father that she left the lantern there, then she would have saved you."

"If not the fire in the barn ruining my career, then it

would have been something else eventually." His words were filled with frustration. "Like today, having to let that horse die."

"That wasn't your fault either."

"Don't you see?" His eyes radiated despair. "I'll always be at risk of becoming the enemy. Because sooner or later I will make a mistake, or I won't be able to fix something—like with Beckett's gelding—and people will hate me."

"The horse was beyond help. No one can be mad at you for that."

"People like to blame someone for their problems. And oftentimes, that happens to be me."

"But everyone also sees how much good you do—"

"All it takes is one person's complaint to undermine me." He reached for his horse's lead line and started toward the barn door. "Once word is out that I couldn't fix Beckett's horse and he thought I could have done more, everyone will start questioning my abilities."

She wanted to stop Thatcher, to shake him, to make him see what a good veterinarian he really was, in spite of a setback or two.

"You want to be with a man who's respected in the community?" He tossed the question over his shoulder. "You won't always get that with me. But you will with Beckett." He stepped into the shadows of the barn and disappeared from her sight.

Even though she was standing in the morning sunshine and wearing her new coat, she couldn't feel the warmth anymore. A chill slithered up her arms and back, and she hugged her arms to her chest.

She didn't believe Thatcher. Even if there were times like today when people disagreed with him, the incidents would fade, especially in light of all the times he succeeded and proved he was willing to help.

But maybe he was telling her all of this because it was his kind way of trying to ease her into putting an end to their marriage. Now that he knew the real Eileen was still out there and waiting to be his bride, why wouldn't he want to meet her and fulfill his promise to her?

A part of Amelia knew she had no right to be with Thatcher, that he deserved to have Eileen if that's who he wanted. But another part of her couldn't keep from wondering why he wasn't willing to keep their marriage. Or at least fight for it a little. Especially since they'd been getting along so well and enjoying being together—at least, she thought they had been.

She supposed it might not be possible to stay together, that the right thing to do was to fulfill her agreement with Beckett and for Thatcher to fulfill his agreement with Eileen. After all, Beckett had demanded Thatcher figure out a way to nullify the marriage.

Of course, their marriage could still be annulled since they hadn't consummated their union. But neither

Beckett nor anyone else in the community knew that their marriage was currently in name only. Would Beckett demand they separate anyway? Perhaps force Thatcher into divorcing her? She wasn't sure what the laws were in the West, but maybe Beckett would simply drag her before the reverend and have another wedding ceremony.

She stared into the open door of the barn, catching sight of Thatcher's outline as he began to unsaddle his horse.

She couldn't deny that she really liked him. In fact, the feelings swirling around inside her were unlike anything she'd ever had for a man. And after the kiss earlier in the morning, she knew that whatever they had growing between them was something special. She didn't want to lose it. Didn't want to lose him.

Why didn't he feel the same way? What was wrong with her that Thatcher didn't want to remain with her? What was her flaw that made people leave her? What was it that her mother hadn't liked? Was it the same thing that Thatcher now saw?

Would she ever be good enough for anyone? Even Beckett?

A tight vise gripped her throat, the pain of rejection— a familiar pain she'd lived with for most of her life. In the same moment, she felt a flutter in her stomach, like that of a bird just starting to fly.

Was it the baby moving?

She cradled a hand over the baby and waited, not sure if she'd actually felt movement or if it was hunger pangs.

The seconds stretched out. She started to lower her hand and shift to walk back to the cabin, but then she felt another flutter, this one more distinct than the last.

A tiny thrill whispered through her, and she splayed her fingers over her abdomen. It was the baby along with the reminder that the baby's happiness and well-being mattered more than her own. She didn't need love. She just needed a good home and a husband to take care of her and the baby. If she had that, then everything would be okay.

If only she could make herself believe it . . .

No one had called on him all day. Not one single person for one single visit.

Thatcher stared unseeingly at the newspaper on his lap. People despised him all over again because, true to his word, Beckett had gone into town and bad-mouthed him to everyone. Jeremy Usher had stopped by earlier in the day to warn Thatcher that the rumors were flying about how he'd purposefully refused to help Beckett's horse and had let him die.

Thatcher blew out a breath, the sound noisy in the silence that was broken only by the crackling fire.

On the sofa across from him, Amelia glanced up from the waist of one of the skirts she was loosening to fit her growing stomach. He didn't meet her gaze, though. He hadn't been able to since yesterday when they'd gotten home from the Noble Ranch and he'd revealed the secret he'd kept from her about his past, the mistake that had forced him to move away from his family and community.

She'd been understanding when he'd told her about Nora and the barn fire. She'd told him the same thing his mother had, that if Nora had really loved him, she wouldn't have let him take the blame. Instead, she would have gone to her father and defended him.

He wasn't sure how his mother had discovered that Nora had been in the barn that night. Maybe she'd just suspected it. Of course, Mother had told Father, and they'd come to his little apartment in town and encouraged him to ask Nora to speak up to her father. Thatcher had refused to pressure Nora in any way and asked his parents not to say anything either. Even though they'd honored his request, they'd warned him that it wouldn't end well.

They'd been right. He'd had to move away in shame.

This time, he'd hoped to be the man of good character Amelia had wanted, someone well-respected in the community. But he had fallen short. And now he was just putting off the inevitable in talking with Amelia about their marriage and how to go about annulling it. Maybe he'd been hanging on to the slim hope that Beckett wouldn't start rumors about the gelding, wouldn't smear his name, wouldn't say anything at all about the bride mix-up. Maybe he'd hoped the situation would all quietly disappear, and he and Amelia could go on with their life as before.

However, Beckett had not only let everyone know about Thatcher's mistakes, meaning no one now wanted his services as a veterinarian, but also spread the rumor that Thatcher had stolen Amelia from him. If people hadn't been upset enough about the first rumor, the second one had nailed the coffin shut.

"Thatcher?" Amelia said tentatively, setting her mending down in her lap. "Should we talk about what we plan to do next?"

She'd asked that last night when they'd been sitting in their spots in front of the fire. He'd answered her that they shouldn't rush into anything and that he wanted time to think about what to do.

She'd nodded and hadn't pushed him to talk, even though the silence was completely foreign to him and their relationship.

She hadn't brought up the issue today either. Even though they hadn't gone anywhere, they'd both kept busy. She'd tended Queen as often as usual, and he'd done all the farm tasks he'd neglected over recent weeks—chopping wood, fixing one of the stall doors, bringing in more hay for the winter, and other boring but necessary duties.

As the day had worn on without a visitor to ask for his help, the last remnants of hope inside him had fizzled into nothing. Now, as he tried to read the newspaper, he could no longer deny the truth. His veterinarian practice had been ruined again.

The other truth was that he loved Amelia, and he wasn't ready to release her from the marriage agreement. He didn't want to lose her. But what right did he have to keep her?

He expelled another tight breath and set the newspaper on the side table.

"You keep sighing," she said softly. "It would probably do us both good to talk about what we should do."

"I know." He slumped over and rested his elbows on his knees while burying his face in his hands. "No one has sought out my services today. That means I'm done here in Summit County." He would become an outcast in this community, the same way he had in Cedar Rapids. Eventually he would have to move on and try to start over again.

"It might just mean none of the animals around here have any major medical needs."

"Or it could be that people have lost confidence in me and my abilities."

"Maybe everyone is busy with Christmas preparations."

Thatcher appreciated that she was trying to make him feel better, but he had to face the reality of his situation. "Animals don't know that it's Christmas and won't take a break from getting sick."

She plucked at a loose thread on the skirt she'd been mending. "We don't know what's really going on, and maybe it's too soon to jump to conclusions."

He wished that were the case. "I've never gone a whole day without being called upon. This is my first."

"I'm sure it has nothing to do with our situation." She didn't look up at him as she tugged at the thread faster.

"According to my friend Jeremy, Beckett went into town yesterday and made it pretty clear to everyone that I wasn't willing to help his horse the way a real veterinarian would. He said why bother having a veterinarian like me if I'm not willing to do things they can't?"

Amelia's pretty brow furrowed above her hazel eyes. "He doesn't really mean it, does he?"

Thatcher shrugged. "Whether he meant it or not, now people are doubting my abilities and my integrity."

She was silent a moment. "Let's hope their doubts pass soon."

"People are taking to heart what Beckett said. He's been around these parts longer than me, and people respect his word."

It was her turn to sigh. "I'm sorry, Thatcher. It's not fair."

The truth was, Beckett was more respected, and since being respected was a quality she valued so highly, then maybe she'd be better off with Beckett.

"So, what would you like to do about everything?" He hadn't wanted to ask her how she wanted to handle the mix-up. But she was right. It was past time to discuss it.

"What do you want to do?" she asked back.

Thatcher had wanted today to bring more clarity. But the only thing it had brought was the confirmation that he wouldn't be the kind of husband she'd wanted. He needed to give her the freedom to choose a different life than the one he had to offer—which would likely result in more times just like this, where a community disliked him and disliked her too as a result.

"I think . . ." He hesitated. "I think . . ."

She set aside the skirt from her lap and then stood abruptly. "It's okay, Thatcher. Just say it—that I'm not good enough for you."

"Not good enough?" He kept his voice gentle and calm, as he'd learned to do in stressful situations with hurt animals. "That's not true at all."

Her beautiful features were creased with distress.

He pushed up from his chair. Every muscle strained to go to her and draw her into his arms. But he had no right to do that anymore. He'd never had the right.

"You can admit it." She lifted her chin as though to brace herself. "I know I'm not the woman you expected or wanted—"

"You're more than I expected." And that was the trouble. She was so much more beautiful and independent and helpful and compassionate and interesting than he'd ever imagined. And now that he'd experienced life with her, he couldn't imagine going a single day without her.

"More?" She scoffed. "Yes, I have more problems and issues and a baby that isn't yours."

"That's not what I mean."

"Eileen will probably be the perfect wife you need. If she were here instead of me, she would have decorated for Christmas, baked you a pie, bought you a present, and made your life more festive." Amelia waved a hand around at the cabin as if that somehow made her point.

But if anything, it only made him all the sadder that he might have to marry Eileen instead. "I don't want someone to decorate or bake or buy me a present. Those things aren't important to me."

"She obviously had qualities that attracted you, that you wanted in a wife, or you wouldn't have sent away for her."

"True enough." He had liked Eileen through her letters. She'd seemed caring and kind and a woman of solid character. He'd thought they shared some similarities and wanted the same things out of life. She probably was a good person and would make a decent wife.

The trouble was that she wasn't Amelia.

"You'll have a good life with her." Her voice was raw.

"You don't know that."

"You're an easy-going person with a big heart. You get along with everyone, and I know you'll get along with her."

Why was Amelia trying so hard to convince him to have Eileen? Was it because she didn't want to hurt his feelings by telling him that she wanted to separate from him? That the disgrace and the dishonor he'd brought on himself were more than she could bear going through again and again?

A sharp pain sliced through his heart. He should have known falling in love with Amelia at first sight was too good to be true.

He couldn't hang on to her if she wanted a different life than the one he could offer her. He would be selfish to try to convince her to stay married when he could only offer her instability and uncertainty.

After all she'd gone through with her first marriage, she deserved better than that, and he couldn't stand in the way of her having a respectable and happy life. As much as he wanted to ask her to stay with him and remain married, he couldn't suggest it. He didn't want her to feel obligated or coerced into anything.

Besides, if they kept their marriage, what would they say to Eileen when she arrived? How could he explain she'd come all that distance—hundreds of miles—but he didn't want her anymore and she would have to go back to New York City?

He couldn't say that. He was too much of a man of honor to absolve himself of his responsibility to her.

She might be willing to look for another husband in Breckenridge. Other men would probably be happy to step in and marry her in his stead. But that wouldn't be fair of him to put that task upon her, especially if she had her heart set on marrying him.

"It was an honest mistake." Thatcher spoke the words almost as if he could convince Eileen. He hadn't meant to betray her, hadn't meant to cause her problems. Was it terrible of him to hope he'd get a letter from her soon letting him know that the reason she hadn't come yet was because she'd changed her mind?

If Beckett insisted on having Amelia, how would everyone in the community respond? Would it cause more scandal? Hurt Amelia's reputation? Bring her more dishonor? Even if Thatcher offered her an annulment and claimed they'd remained chaste, they had been married for close to two weeks, and people would probably speculate and gossip about them.

"I agree that the mix-up was a mistake," Amelia said quietly. "So what do we do next? How do we right the wrong?"

What was the best thing to do for Amelia? Her happiness and her secure future were more important than anything else. But what would make her the happiest? Breaking off their union so she didn't have to live with his dishonor? Or breaking off their union and causing her dishonor anyway?

"What is the right thing, Thatcher?"

"I don't know. I don't think there is an easy or right answer."

As she lifted her gaze to his, something in her eyes seemed to reach out and plead with him not to hurt her. She'd been hurt too many times already in her short life. This time, he had to do whatever he could to make sure she wasn't harmed again, even if that decision meant he would lose her and bring himself pain in the process.

Her hand trembled as she lowered herself back into her chair. "Could we wait until after Christmas to make the decision on what to do?"

Christmas was in only two days. Could they have until the New Year? But even as the question pushed to the tip of his tongue, he knew they couldn't delay until then. The longer they lived together, the harder it would be to annul their marriage without causing her damage.

"Okay." He ought to ride over and talk to Beckett today. But he would take two more days with Amelia. "I say let's enjoy the holiday and then figure out what to do afterward."

She leaned back, the stiffness easing from her body. "Thank you."

"I'll take as much time with you as I can get." The

words slipped out before he could censor them.

Her eyes swung back to his, her long lashes framing her wide eyes. Was that a flicker of hope?

Was it possible she'd begun to care about him too? Was it possible she didn't want to leave him but felt obligated to fulfill her commitment to Beckett?

He didn't know. But he'd bought himself two more days. Two days to pray for a Christmas miracle.

Amelia awoke to the scent of something sweet in the air. She blinked her eyes open to the soft glow of dawn. The tip of her nose was cold and her breath frosty in the chill of the bedroom air, but her body was thoroughly warm.

As more wakefulness seeped through her, she became aware that she was warm for two reasons. One, her feet in her thick wool socks were pressed against a warming stone—a warming stone that was still heated and had obviously been tucked under the covers recently. Two, several extra blankets were tucked around her securely— blankets that hadn't been there when she'd fallen asleep last night.

She couldn't hold back a smile. A blast of arctic air had blown in with the winter storm yesterday. With the frigid temperature, the stove and fireplace hadn't been able to keep the whole place heated. Thatcher had obviously recognized how cold the bedroom had gotten and had been in and taken care of her the way he always did.

Just as soon as the smile came, it faded away. Today was Christmas Day, which meant tomorrow they would have to talk again about their marriage mix-up. She didn't even want to think about it. But after the past two days of ignoring it, the deadline was fast approaching.

She had to ignore it for today too. She couldn't let the fears and uncertainties about her future—their future—infringe on her enjoyment of her last day with Thatcher.

She didn't want it to be her last day, but how could she prove to him that she could be enough?

She'd wanted to show him over the past two days that she was a good wife, a perfect wife, so that he wouldn't push her aside for another woman. While he'd been busy with projects around the farm, she'd finished cleaning the house and had baked a pecan pie—although the filling had spilled over and burned. She'd cut pine boughs and hung them on the mantel with red ribbon she'd found in a trunk. She'd created a centerpiece for the kitchen table with more pine boughs and red ribbon. And she'd decorated the lanterns with sprigs of holly.

Yesterday they'd cut down a small pine tree in the woods near the cabin and brought it in and made it festive with strings of popcorn and berries along with bows of the red ribbon tied on the ends of branches.

He'd complimented her on how pretty everything

looked, and he'd enjoyed every bite of his pie. He'd told her numerous times how much he appreciated her help with tidying and cleaning and organizing. And he'd been as sweet to her as always.

But had she won him over? Or did she need more time to show him that she could be enough?

Today would be the last day to do it. If they were able to brave the cold and the snow, they were planning to go over to his cousin's house for Christmas dinner. The snow had been blowing too hard last night for them to make it to the Christmas Eve service in Breckenridge, but from the silence outside, it sounded like the wind had died down today.

He'd only made two veterinarian calls over the past couple of days. Even though both had been at the same ranch near Frisco, at least it had been something. Thatcher had said the family probably hadn't yet heard the rumors about him, which was why they'd requested his services. She hoped that wasn't the whole truth and that people would soon forgive and forget any grudges they might have against him.

In her effort to show him she could be a good wife, she'd declined to go with him on the visits even though she'd wanted to accompany him, not only to help him but also to spend time with him. Instead, she'd stayed at the cabin and cooked and cleaned and done laundry.

What else could she do to show him that she cared

about their marriage? The truth was, she didn't want it to end. She didn't want to be with any other man. She only wanted him.

But she couldn't just come out and say that and put pressure on him to stay with her. Not when he was such a good man and wanted to do what was right and straighten out the mix-up for everyone.

She shifted so she was facing the bedroom doorway and could see into the main room. The area glowed with low light, and she could hear the clanking of a pan.

Was he making breakfast? Was that what she was smelling?

Her heart swelled with all the feelings that had been settling there since marrying him. He was so caring. In fact, he spoiled her. The warming stone and the extra blankets were proof of that.

She rested her head against her pillow and closed her eyes, savoring the warmth that was swirling around inside her chest. She had to admit that being with him recently had been bringing a warmth all of its own. All she knew was that she loved seeing his smile, loved hearing him talk, and loved simply being with him.

Even now, her body tingled with a strange need to be with him. Although she didn't want to leave her warm cocoon, she pushed the covers off. As the cold air hit her, she shuddered. She'd opted not to wear her thin nightgown last night and had worn layers of clothing.

Even so, she wrapped one of the blankets around her shoulders before stepping into her boots and crossing to the door.

As she exited the bedroom, she stopped short at the sight that met her. The candle centerpiece was lit and two places set at the table with what appeared to be a present on one of the plates. Thatcher stood in front of the stove and was cooking eggs.

Somehow he'd heard her, and he shifted, offering her one of his easy smiles. "Merry Christmas, sweetheart." His hair was mussed and one of his suspenders down, but he'd never looked better, especially with the heavy layer of scruff that he hadn't shaved over the past couple of days.

"Merry Christmas." She let her gaze drift to his chest and then his arms, both of which strained against his shirt. The warmth inside fanned a few degrees hotter. How was it that he looked more handsome every day? Or was she just growing more attracted to him?

His smile tilted up higher on one side. "I can tell you're hungry."

She was staring at him as if he were on the menu for breakfast. Could he see the hunger for him in her expression? Or was he referring to the meal?

He waggled his brows playfully before turning back to the pan.

Her heart tumbled over itself in a dizzying spin. Yes, he'd noticed her ogling him and was teasing her, and she should be embarrassed by it. But strangely, she wasn't. Did she want him to know of her hunger for him? That she was attracted? That she desired him?

This hunger, attraction, desire—that was what he'd wanted to develop between them when he'd talked to her about waiting to share the marriage bed. She understood that now in a way she hadn't previously because she'd never experienced this kind of desire before.

If she showed him more of her desire today, would that finally win him over?

He nodded toward the loaf on the back burner. "I warmed the Christmas stollen I purchased in Frisco yesterday."

"That must have been what I smelled in bed." She breathed in the scent of sweet citrus and almond. The aroma of freshly brewed coffee lingered in the air too.

"My mother made stollen every year at Christmas, and so when I saw it, I thought it would help me not miss them so much this year."

At the wistfulness in his tone, she crossed to him. It was his first Christmas without his family, because even when he'd been in school, he'd always traveled home at Christmas over his breaks. They'd talked about that last night, about missing their loved ones and how even though he had his cousin Lee in the area, that didn't make up for missing his parents and siblings.

As she stepped behind him, she laid a hand on his

back, similar to the gentle way he often did with her. "What can I do to help?"

"It's all ready." He lifted the pan off the burner and placed it on the warmer at the back of the stove next to the loaf of stollen.

"I could pour the coffee."

He tossed aside the towel he'd been using to move the hot pan, then pivoted and placed his hands on her hips before she could back away.

She nearly swooned at the pressure of his hands there, the strength of his fingers and yet the gentleness of his hold. She couldn't deny that she adored it whenever he held her this way. He'd only done it a few times, but with each successive time, she loved it even more.

"All you have to do is go sit down," he said with a smile that made her pulse stutter. "I want to serve you breakfast this morning."

"I can carry something—"

He lifted a finger to her lips and cut her off.

Of course, then she was much too conscious of his finger against her lips—the hard length, the calloused skin, and the sweet taste of almond glaze.

Without thinking, she licked his finger, getting a small taste of the glaze.

His smile disappeared, and his eyes darkened.

What had she done? Had she really been so bold as to lick him?

He didn't immediately move his finger away, but his gaze dropped to her mouth.

She needed to apologize, didn't she? Or what if she didn't? Because she wasn't sorry, and she actually wanted to do it again. What did she have to lose? If she didn't show him that she was attracted to him, then tomorrow would come and he would send her on her way. But if she made today all about letting him know that she did feel something for him, then maybe he would have second thoughts.

Giving herself no chance to object, she stuck out her tongue and licked his finger again, this time more slowly.

The hand that remained on her hip tightened. Then, as if her licks had somehow unlocked a territory that had previously been forbidden, he traced his finger across her bottom lip.

Oh my. The heat inside radiated out, sending tight, pleasurable waves through her belly.

He drew his finger back across her lower lip, as though he hadn't gotten enough of the feel of it the first time. Then he traced her upper lip.

The waves inside her belly crashed again, harder.

His pupils widened, turning his eyes darker with desire.

She'd noticed his desire a time or two when he hadn't realized she'd caught him watching her. And each time, seeing that craving had filled her with wonder. But today, now, it sent more than just pleasure through her body. It sent an echo of her own desire—desire she didn't quite understand but that she knew had everything to do with him, because suddenly she wanted to be close to him, to hold him, and to press against him. In fact, she wasn't sure that she would feel satisfied or complete until she did.

Of course, being together like that wasn't possible and wouldn't be right. Not when they hadn't decided on the course of their relationship and whether they were obligated to remain with their original choices of partners or if they were now obligated to stay together.

She didn't realize she'd stopped breathing until he lifted his finger away from her lips. Then she expelled a short burst, almost of protest.

Would he at least kiss her? There wouldn't be anything wrong with sharing another kiss, would there?

Before she could suggest it and embarrass herself, he was rotating her and guiding her to the table. He pulled out her bench, waited for her to sit, then pushed her in. "No peeking at the present." He winked at her as he started back to the stove.

For a few minutes, he was busy dishing up the eggs he'd cooked, slicing them each a generous piece of stollen, then pouring coffee. While they ate, they shared memories of past Christmases, and he made her laugh, as usual, with the tales of his boyhood mischief.

When they were finished and their mugs empty, she jumped up before he could and poured them each a second cup. As she returned to the table after putting the coffeepot back on the stove, he reached out and snagged her hand.

"Did I tell you yet today how beautiful you are?" He intertwined his fingers with hers as his gaze lingered over her face, caressing her forehead and cheek and then her chin and neck.

She loved his compliments. He was always so sincere, and she knew he truly believed she was beautiful even though she'd just crawled out of bed and hadn't taken any care with her appearance.

His laced fingers slid into hers more deeply, and then he tugged her closer. "I have a present for you."

"You already gave me a coat. That was more than enough."

"I got it on the same day but made myself wait for Christmas for this one."

"You can't give me anything more." Her protest was weak, though, because he was still drawing her forward until she bumped into him where he was seated on the bench. Then before she knew what was happening, he was pulling her down onto his lap.

"Thatcher." She laughed at his silliness and tried to stand back up.

Not letting her get away, he wrapped an arm around

her waist and settled her more securely on his lap. "Open it right here, where I can see you."

"You can see me if I sit in my spot."

"I can see you better here."

He released his hold of her hand and swiped up the present from near her plate on the table. He set it on her lap, then combed some of her long loose strands back over her shoulder before brushing a thumb over her upper arm.

She loved his touch, loved his fingers in her hair, loved his thumb on her arm. It didn't feel intrusive or demanding. Instead she felt cherished, as if she was precious to him, a treasure he wanted to both protect and admire.

Sitting on his legs like this was a new experience for her as well. Even though she was slightly embarrassed by it, she didn't want to get up. She could admit she relished the closeness and the warmth of his presence. And with her growing attraction, she found the little things about him appealing, like the veins running through his strong hands, or the scruff that covered his chin and continued down to his neck, or the leathery lines next to his eyes.

His head was only inches from hers, and she wanted to lean into him, press a kiss to his messy hair, run her fingers through it, and then kiss his neck.

At the brazenness of her thoughts, heat circled through her and rose to her face.

"Open it," he persisted softly, his voice near, making her insides tumble.

She fingered the pretty white bow and the brown paper covering the small box. Even without opening it, she realized she was happy—happy sitting with him, happy being on his lap, happy with his breakfast, happy that he was giving her a present even though he'd already given her the coat.

She started to untie the bow. The truth was that she was really happy for the first time in her life because she was with him . . . because she loved him.

Her fingers halted even as her heart began to race with the realization of her love for Thatcher. She wasn't quite sure how she knew that it was love, but she did.

Before timidity could creep in, she reached up both hands, cupped his face, and forced him to look at her. "I love you, Thatcher."

At her declaration, his eyes widened, and the blue filled with warmth and sunshine.

She didn't want to wait to hear what he would say in response. She didn't want him to feel obligated to make any declarations in return. Instead, she leaned in and pressed her lips to his, needing to show him how much she truly cared about him and how loath she was to let him go.

Amelia loved him.

Thatcher's chest swelled with a swift current of emotions he couldn't name but that brought a lump into his throat.

She loved him. And now she was kissing him.

Her lips plied his shyly and sweetly, as though she wanted to kiss him to express her love but didn't want to overstep herself.

He needed her to know he would always, always welcome her kisses, that any time she wanted to give him one, he would accept it.

Wrapping his arms around her more securely, he angled in and fused his mouth with hers, hoping to reassure her he would take everything she offered. He didn't care about the tough decisions about their future that still loomed ahead. He didn't care that he was making his life more complicated. And he didn't care that everything was so uncertain.

All that mattered was her. She was more important than his career as a veterinarian, more important than the approval of the community, more important than keeping the peace with Beckett or even Eileen when she arrived.

If Amelia loved him and wanted to be with him, then he'd sacrifice everything to be with her. Because the truth was, he loved her too.

He delved into their kiss with all of that love and passion . . . and the delight of knowing she was his. After the past few days of agonizing over the marriage muddle, the doubts fled to the back corners of his mind, and he basked in the light of her love.

Her arms slipped up and wound around his neck, and she moved into the kiss deeply too. Her lips were just as full and delectable as they had been previously. But somehow this time, the touch seared him all the way to his core, sparking a fire inside that flared to life and sent heat sizzling through his veins.

He didn't know what would happen tomorrow or the next day or the next month. But he had Amelia, and she was more than he ever could have asked for in a wife, in the companion and friend who would walk alongside him in the journey of life.

He enjoyed being with her more than he ever had any other person, which was saying a lot since he never turned down an opportunity to be around people. There was something so attentive about her, as if she was invested in everything he had to say. She also wasn't afraid to speak her mind and tell him if she didn't agree with him. And she was deeply compassionate—that was easy to see in how she'd given up her life for her father and his farm, how she cared so much about her unborn babe, and how she even cared about the helpless animals that no one else wanted.

As if sensing the deepening desire within him, she pressed her body to his and wound her fingers more firmly into his hair. Her kiss turned suddenly harder and hungrier with a need that only added fuel to the flames raging in his body and fanned his own needs into consuming heat.

Desire pulsed through him. He wanted to sweep her up and take her to the bedroom and forget all about the presents. A groan pushed for release, but he swallowed it and forced himself to stay on his bench.

Even if he was allowing himself to acknowledge this love that had swiftly taken root and grown between them, deep inside, he knew they had to make things right with both Beckett and Eileen before they moved forward with their marriage.

Yes, it was clear that he couldn't relinquish Amelia. But he had to make sure she was aware that staying with him would possibly bring her a life of hardship. He needed her to know what she was getting herself into with him.

"Amelia," he whispered, breaking their kiss.

She chased after his lips, catching his mouth again, and tugging him back.

This time he did groan, her desire and her boldness only adding power to the flames burning inside him.

He kissed her again, this time wildly, almost frantically, as if at any moment she would be ripped from him, and he would never have the opportunity to kiss her again.

It wasn't true, was it?

What if she decided that she couldn't endure a lifetime of the uncertainty that came with his work? What if that would be too much disgrace for her to bear?

He had to know.

This time he broke the kiss and stood. In the same motion, he set her on the bench he'd vacated and gently pried her arms loose from his neck. Before she could protest or find a way to wrap him back up in another kiss, he paced away from her until he found himself standing in front of the fireplace.

His breathing was labored, and he combed his fingers through his messy hair. Everything in him wanted to turn around and make sure she was okay. But he knew if he looked at her, he'd only be drawn right back into her arms and into another kiss.

Before he kissed her again, he had to make certain this marriage was what she wanted.

"Amelia," he started again. "I want you to know that I love you more than anything, that I think I fell in love with you on the first day I met you."

Her breathing was ragged too, but at his declaration, it seemed to even out, as if his words brought her reassurance.

"Yes, I love you." He needed her to know there was no question about his love. "It's because I love you that I want to make sure you are well aware of the problems that will come with being married to me."

The bench scraped as she stood, and her footsteps padded against the floorboard.

He had to say everything before she came to him and silenced him with her touch or another kiss. He pivoted and held out a hand to halt her progression.

She took another step, then stopped. Her face was flushed, her lips swollen, and her hazel eyes bright with tenderness.

Heaven help him. He stiffened his shoulders to keep himself from stalking back to her and kissing her senseless.

"I realize you will be maligned at times," she said softly, "but it doesn't matter—"

"It does matter." His statement came out more passionate than he intended. But he needed her to understand the seriousness of choosing to be with him. "As you saw from what happened with Beckett's horse, one decision can cost me my career."

"I don't care about that."

"But I don't want you to be ostracized from the community like you were with Charles."

She cocked her head and studied him for a long second. "Thatcher, you are not like Charles. Not even a little. Charles was selfish and cold and uncaring and deserved to be ostracized and disliked. But you . . . you are kind and giving and friendly to everyone you see."

"That doesn't change the fact that people will turn against me." He appreciated her encouragement, but sometimes all it took was one person spreading one bad rumor to ruin someone.

"People might talk for a little while, but your true character will speak louder eventually."

"That didn't happen the last time and might not this time either."

Her face took on a determined, even a fierce look. "If people cannot see through the rumors to what a good and decent man you are, then they don't deserve to have you in this community."

He inwardly smiled at her sweet words of defense. But that still didn't change the situation. "I don't want to put you through having a disgraced husband again."

"Again?" Her brows rose. "Thatcher, I will gladly be ostracized with you. Because I see the caring and compassionate man that you truly are and will stand beside you no matter what."

She was amazing, and he longed to have that kind of support—the support he hadn't had from Nora, who'd cut him out of her life when her father had demanded she call off the engagement.

"Because you're a man of true integrity and character," she continued, "I'm honored to be your wife, no matter what anyone else says. And even if the truth about who you really are gets buried beneath lies, I still know who you are and will always respect you and don't care about their misguided opinions."

Once again, Amelia's words were reminiscent of what his mother had told him right before he'd left, when he'd been hugging her goodbye. She'd told him she believed in him and would always love and respect him, no matter what anyone else said about him.

Amelia's belief in him was just as strong, if not stronger. If he'd allowed himself any doubts, they were now gone. She was the one for him. And if she was willing to stick with him through all the adversities life would bring them, then he would do his best to be worthy of her.

"If you're sure you'll have me," he started again, "then I'm sure I'll have you."

She didn't answer. Instead, she bolted forward and raced across the room toward him. As she reached him, she flung herself upon him.

In the same instant, he wrapped his arms around her and drew her into a tight embrace. He squeezed his eyes closed. This. This was what he wanted. Her and only her.

Her arms slid around him, and she rested her head against his chest. "I don't want anyone else but you, Thatcher."

He pressed a hard kiss to the top of her head. "Then you're not at all curious to know more about Beckett?"

"No, not after how he handled himself."

"So I'm still your favored cowboy?"

She snuggled into his chest. "Far and above my favored."

"Good, because I'm not sure I would have been able to give you up to him."

"And I won't be able to give you up to Eileen."

Now that he had Amelia in his arms again, he wanted to mesh his mouth with hers and kiss her all day . . . and all night. With as much passion as there was sizzling between them, he was pretty sure she would agree they were both attracted to one another and ready for the marriage bed—at least, he was.

Yet even though he was eager for more and suspected she was too, the honorable part of him wanted to make sure he settled things with both Beckett and Eileen before letting himself get carried away with Amelia.

He sighed. "As much as I would like to kiss you again right here and now, I think we both owe Beckett and

Eileen explanations before we take the next step forward in our marriage."

She seemed to hesitate, then her arms tightened around him. "That's one of the things I love about you. That you want to do the right thing even when it's difficult."

The tension he hadn't realized was in his shoulders loosened.

"We'll need to communicate with them both soon, though." Her voice was muffled against him. "Because I want to kiss you as often and as long as I want."

"Do you now?" He couldn't keep the happiness from his tone as he teased her.

"I do." She pulled back and smiled up at him, such a wide and happy smile that he was sure he'd never been happier in his entire life.

19

"Oh, Thatcher." She lifted the bracelet out of the box. "It's stunning." The gold band was studded with several delicate jewels and a dangling button with an engraving of a horse.

Sitting beside her on the sofa, Thatcher lifted her hand and placed a kiss on her wrist. "May I?" he asked as he took the bracelet.

She nodded and let him wrap it around her, marveling that he'd given her something so beautiful. No one ever had before. Her father had never had the money to buy her anything so nice, and even though Charles had been wealthy, he'd been stingy with what he'd given her.

"My mother's father was a veterinarian." Thatcher gently hooked the ends of the bracelet together. "She went with him everywhere, just like you do with me. And he gifted her with a bracelet just like this, adding engraved buttons to it each year with the animals she'd helped to save."

"That's lovely."

He fingered the engraving. "This is to represent Queen, the first animal you helped to save."

"Really?"

"Yes, and there's room for many more in the days ahead."

"Then you want me to continue going on calls with you?"

"I wouldn't have it any other way. I missed having you come with me on the last couple of calls."

As his eyes met hers, the warmth and love in the depths of the blue made everything about this Christmas better than any she'd ever had. They'd finished breakfast a short while ago, and she'd made quick work of cleaning it up while he went out to the barn to tend to the animals. She'd also changed into a nice gown and styled her hair in preparation for their Christmas celebration at his cousin's.

"Are you sure you want me tagging along? Would you rather have a wife who stays at home and takes care of everything here, like tidying the house and cooking you warm meals?"

He caressed the sensitive spot just inside her wrist, and his eyes crinkled at the corners just the way she loved. "I'd much rather have your company and help than a tidy house and a warm meal."

Was it possible she could be enough for Thatcher?

"You sure you won't eventually get tired of me and our messy house someday and leave me behind?"

He paused and studied her face for several long seconds then swept a strand of her loose hair back from her cheek. "You told me I wasn't like Charles. Now it's my turn to remind you that I'm also not like your mother."

"My mother?"

"You're not to blame for your mother leaving you. You have to accept that your mother was the one with the problem, not you."

In her head, she knew that, but it was much harder to make her heart believe the truth, especially when she'd spent so much of her life wondering what was wrong with her that her mother didn't love her. "I wasn't enough for her, and sometimes I can't help but wonder if I'll be enough for you."

"You are way more than enough." His eyes turned serious. "But none of us are perfect. So even when you make mistakes or have a bad day or whatever happens, I'll keep on loving you, because that's what real love does."

She tried to absorb what he was saying, but it seemed too good to be true.

"I won't leave you, Amelia." His words were so soft and so sincere that they brought the sting of tears to the backs of her eyes. "You said you would stay with me no matter how tarnished my reputation might become. And

I would like to vow to you that I will stay with you too, through everything that may come our way."

She sniffled and then launched herself against him, wrapping him in another hug. Yes, she was grateful for his support and his ability to recognize what she needed to hear. But she couldn't deny that she was using every excuse she could find to touch him.

They'd agreed that they wouldn't move any further along in their marital intimacy out of respect for Beckett and Eileen. But that didn't mean she had to resist hugging Thatcher, did it? Or stealing small kisses? Or caressing him in passing?

The trouble was, every time she held him, she had a harder time letting go of him and keeping her hands to herself. If she wasn't careful, she might get carried away, and she didn't want to cause Thatcher to do anything that might compromise his integrity. And she didn't want to do anything to compromise hers either.

With a measure of restraint she hadn't realized she had, she released him, but not before breathing in his scent, which contained the almond sweetness of the stollen.

He'd done so much for her that she wanted him to know how much she appreciated him. Even though she hadn't been able to purchase him a gift, she had been thinking about what she could give him . . . and there was one thing.

"Just a minute." She hopped up from the sofa and hurried into the bedroom. After rummaging through her bags, she found what she was looking for, then wrapped it in a scrap of linen and added a red ribbon from those she'd found when decorating the cabin.

Before she lost her courage, she returned to the sofa where he was waiting, sat down, and placed the gift between them. "This is for you."

His grin came out as faithfully as always—a grin that she was falling in love with every bit as much as she was falling in love with him. "I didn't realize you'd gone shopping—"

"It's not new like the bracelet." Maybe she'd been rash to think she could give him something used.

"If it's from you, then I'll love it. I promise."

"It's definitely not as nice as what you gave me."

"That doesn't matter." He skimmed her fingers.

As usual, the barest of his touches made her keenly aware of him—of his calluses, of the strength of his fingers, and of the way he could be so gentle with her.

"It's not the cost or the newness that makes the gift special. It's the giver and the love that make it meaningful."

He was right. It wasn't about the cost. It was about the meaning. "It means everything to me, which is why I want you to have it."

He picked up the gift solemnly. As he began to untie

the red ribbon, he flashed glances her way, as though gauging her emotions and making sure she was okay.

Oh, she loved him for his sweetness and concern. She was amazed at how quickly and thoroughly her love had come about. And she was surprised that he felt the same way so quickly and thoroughly. His words of love a short while ago during breakfast still held her heart captive.

Yes, they might have a difficult road ahead in explaining their marriage mix-up to the community. They would have to apologize to both Beckett and Eileen. But in the end, she was relieved Thatcher wanted to stay with her and fight for their relationship.

He peeled the folds of linen back to reveal a silver pocket watch on a silver chain.

"It belonged to my father." Her throat closed up as she pictured her father pulling the watch out of his pocket and checking it every night so that they went to bed on time without fail.

As a single father, he'd done the best he could to raise her and love her. It hadn't been easy for him to lose his wife and then take care of a tiny daughter while he ran a demanding dairy farm.

He'd persevered, and even in the end, when threatened with losing his farm, he'd encouraged her to marry Charles because he thought she would have a more secure future with Charles, away from the farm and away from its problems. She'd sensed that he hadn't wanted to let her go, that he would miss her, that he would be lonely without her. But he'd thought he was giving her a better life.

She hadn't wanted to leave the farm or her father, but she'd wanted to repay him for his many years of taking care of her and thought she could do that by giving him the farm.

Whatever the case, the watch was all she had left of him besides her memories.

"Thank you, Amelia." Thatcher fingered the silver case that covered the face of the watch. "I'm honored to have it."

"It's the only thing of his that I was able to get. I took it out of the coroner's office without Charles realizing I'd done so."

Thatcher was silent, turning the watch over, then opening and closing it. When he glanced up at her, his eyes held sadness. "I'm sorry this is all you got. Charles should have allowed you to have anything you wanted of your father's."

"I know my father would love you and want you to have it." A tightness gripped her throat. "More importantly, I want you to have it because it's a symbol of my devotion to you, that I will love you every minute throughout all time."

His eyes turned glassy. "That's about the sweetest thing you could ever say to me."

"I mean it."

He opened it again and watched it for a moment. Then he closed it, tucked it in his vest pocket, and met her gaze again, his eyes filled with so much love that she could hardly breathe. "It's the best gift I've ever been given."

"Really?"

"Well, there is one gift that's better." His lips quirked with the beginning of a smile.

"And what might that be?"

"You and the gift of your love that you gave me today."

"Merry Christmas, Thatcher."

"Merry Christmas to you too, Amelia." He leaned in and stole a kiss that was much too short.

As he pulled back, her chest burned with the need for more. But she kept her hands folded in her lap, resisting the urge to kiss him again.

How much longer could she keep resisting? She would just have to pray for a peaceful and swift resolution to their marriage mix-up, although she feared the coming storm would be neither peaceful nor swift.

Thatcher enjoyed spending Christmas with Lee and his family. The time with them took some of the sting out of being away from his parents and siblings.

Of course, being with Amelia anywhere and at any time made his life brighter too, especially now that they'd determined how to proceed with their future together. She'd made it clear that she wanted to be with him, had declared her love, and had even given him her father's watch as a sign of her commitment. He couldn't have asked for more.

Now he just had to figure out a way out of the mess that their marriage had caused.

"So you're telling me you both have different matches that are still waiting to marry you?" Lee asked as he puffed on his pipe at the table after they'd finished the last of the wild grouse along with the potatoes and other delicious side dishes Dot had prepared. A wisp of a woman compared to Lee, she sat in the chair beside her husband and was sipping a cup of tea, seemingly in no hurry to begin the clean-up of the meal and instead relishing the time with company.

"That's what we're telling you." Thatcher set down the two-year-old tyke who had climbed onto his lap after dinner and was now wiggling his way free to go play with carved wooden animals that his older brother had dumped out on the floor nearby.

Lee and his boys had the stocky Hoyt build. A few years older than Thatcher, Lee had grown up on an Iowa farm not far from Thatcher's since their dads were brothers. But Lee had red hair—or at least, what was left of it after losing most of it over the past couple of years to a receding hairline.

Lee had initially come to Colorado to try his hand at mining and getting rich quick. When he'd failed at that, he'd opened a fishing and hunting business, selling fresh fish and game as well as supplies for fishermen and hunters in the area.

He was doing well for himself and had built a fine home attached to his store in Breckenridge. He and Dot seemed happy to be in the West, even though they were so far away from home. Maybe having each other and having their own family made it easier.

Thatcher was reclining in his chair beside Amelia, who was holding Lee and Dot's youngest child, another boy who had been born over the summer. Amelia had been interested in the babe all the while they'd been eating and visiting, probably thinking about her own child.

Now that Thatcher had cleared up his confusion about when Amelia had married and conceived, he'd helped her calculate approximately when the baby was due. They guessed likely in May. They'd also decided to be honest and let everyone know she was a widow and the baby's father was her previous husband.

On the horse ride over, they'd also agreed to tell Lee and Dot everything about their situation. Thankfully, the young couple had been sympathetic and hadn't passed judgment. Thatcher didn't expect the revelation of the mail-order-bride mishap to go so well with everyone else. But at least their version of the tale would soon be out there for everyone to hear instead of just Beckett's rumors.

"No one meant to make the mistake." Lee leveled a long look at Thatcher through the haze of pipe smoke. "So it seems that your intended can't hold you responsible for what happened."

"Unfortunately, Beckett's already made the accusation that I stole Amelia from him." Thatcher's shoulders tensed at just the thought of the confrontation that was sure to come when he went to Beckett and told him he was keeping Amelia. Would they have a fight? Were duels legal in Colorado? If they were, Beckett would probably challenge him to one. Or maybe the foreman would throw Amelia over his shoulder and steal her away.

If that happened, Thatcher might be forced to hurt Beckett. Either way, he had the feeling their next meeting wouldn't be civil.

Amelia laid a hand on Thatcher's arm. She'd obviously sensed his wariness, and now her eyes met his, and she seemed to be silently reassuring him that nothing would separate them.

He picked up her hand and kissed the back of it and prayed she was right.

At the kiss, a soft glow filled her eyes, turning the hazel more green than brown. Her lips curved up just a little, and she sidled closer to him, leaning her head against his shoulder.

His chest expanded with love that couldn't be contained. It rose into his throat, tightening his airway. He bent in and pressed a kiss to the top of her head.

In return, she tucked her free hand into the crook of his arm and expelled a soft breath that seemed to be filled with contentment.

Thatcher couldn't stop himself from pressing one more kiss against her head. "I love you," he whispered.

"I love you too," she whispered back.

He was surprised at how gratified he felt, given all the problems that awaited him in the coming days. Maybe, with the right person by his side, the dark valleys wouldn't be so difficult to walk through.

As he settled back again, he noticed the silence in the room, only broken by the chatter of the boys playing on the floor nearby. He glanced up to find Lee and Dot watching him and Amelia with wide eyes.

Thatcher was tempted to squirm under their scrutiny. Instead, he did what he was good at—he initiated more conversation. "So if Eileen shows up now or in the spring expecting to marry me, I'm thinking I'll offer to pay for her to return east. It only seems fair."

Lee's gaze bounced back and forth between him and Amelia. Then he met his wife's gaze, and they both smiled.

"What?" Thatcher asked, offering a smile of his own. "What's so humorous?"

"Nothing," Dot offered.

"You are," Lee said at the same time.

"I'm humorous?"

"No." Dot lightly slapped Lee's arm. "You're adorable, Thatcher. You and Amelia are adorable together. And it's very clear you were made for each other."

"Really?" Thatcher loved hearing that. He didn't need the affirmation, because he already loved Amelia more than his own life. But he appreciated that someone else was noticing what he had—that Amelia was perfect for him.

Lee's expression turned playful. "Who knew you'd be such a softie?"

Was he a softie? Maybe he was. But that was okay with him.

"I love the way you interact with each other." Dot's smile widened. "It's obvious you're really in love."

Lee nodded. "Yep, more than with any other woman you've been with."

Lee had lived in Iowa before Thatcher had left for college, when he'd been young and naïve and claiming to be in love with a new woman every other week.

"Speaking of other women"—Dot rose from her chair—"we got a letter from my folks earlier in the week, and they said to tell you they're happy Nora confessed that her lantern started the barn fire."

Thatcher's racing thoughts came to an abrupt halt. "What?"

Dot was crossing to a sideboard. "Apparently she told one of her girlfriends, and the word started to spread around the community."

"When was this?" And why hadn't anyone written from home and told him the news?

Lee finished taking another puff on his pipe. "From the way Dot's folks tell it, Nora made the confession last month."

Dot pulled open a drawer, fumbled inside, and retrieved a letter. "Here's the letter from my mother.

You're welcome to read it."

Thatcher's mind raced with the implications of such news. If Nora had told everyone she'd left the lantern that had caused the fire, then he would be absolved of the blame for killing the prize horses as well as destroying the barn. He wouldn't have the shame hanging over his head any longer.

Dot crossed back toward him, holding out the letter. "I'm sure you'll get the news from your family soon. A letter or two is probably on its way and will arrive any day."

Amelia's words from earlier echoed in his head: *People might talk for a little while, but your true character will speak louder eventually.*

If that was happening back in Iowa, could he hope it would happen here too? That people would let his character speak for itself, that they would understand he cared about them and their animals even when he couldn't save every creature?

He could only hope that was the case.

Quietly, he skimmed Dot's letter until he reached the paragraph about Nora and how, after pressure from the rumors that were circling, she'd admitted to leaving the lantern that had started the barn fire that had killed her father's horses.

Her father had apparently been embarrassed and apologized for blaming Thatcher and ruining his veterinarian practice in Cedar Rapids. From the sounds of things, many former clients had come forward and spoken highly of Thatcher and all he'd done to help them.

When Thatcher finished reading, he passed the letter to Amelia, who read it, then wordlessly returned it to Dot. Then Amelia tilted up and brushed a kiss across his jaw. "We won't always get the justice we're due, but it's sure nice when it happens."

"Very nice," Dot echoed. "Guess that means you can go on back home to Iowa if you've got a mind to."

Thatcher kissed Amelia's forehead. He hadn't anticipated ever having the option of returning home, had thought he'd be an outcast forever. But maybe he ought to consider the possibility if his reputation was irreparable here in Breckenridge.

"What do you think, sweetheart?" he asked. "Do you have your heart set on staying here in the high country?"

"I've got my heart set on staying with you wherever you go." Her response was quick and earnest. Even so, he could tell it wasn't complete, that she had more to say.

"But . . .?"

She settled her head back against his arm while adjusting her hold on the baby. "No buts. I just want to be with you. That's all that matters, even here, where it still may take some time for people to see that you're not God and won't be saving all the animals. But you're a godly man who lives an upright and righteous life and loves people generously."

She was right again. He couldn't run off whenever someone called into question his abilities. In doing so, he was taking the cowardly way instead of staying strong and showing that he had nothing to hide and nothing to be ashamed of.

"Whatever you decide," she whispered, "I'll be by your side."

And that was really all that mattered. He had her and her love. It was enough to get him through any hardship . . . at least, he hoped it was enough to get them through the coming confrontation with Beckett without anyone getting hurt.

21

"'I am sincerely sorry for any problems or issues this mix-up may cause you.'" Amelia read aloud the letter Thatcher had just finished penning to Eileen. "'I promise to do everything within my power to make sure you are taken care of until other arrangements can be made for your well-being.'"

Thatcher remained at the kitchen table, his pen in hand, his brow furrowed above troubled eyes. "What do you think? Does it sound caring enough, or should I add something else?"

Amelia scanned the one-page sheet, the ink barely dry. "I think you're being as responsible as you can be in offering to help her make arrangements to return to the East or to help her until she can find another marriageable prospect here."

"Then it's fair?"

"I think so." Amelia carefully considered the letter to

Eileen, putting herself in the poor woman's place. What would she have done if she'd arrived to find her groom—the one she'd been writing to for months—had accidentally married another woman?

She supposed she would have questioned whether the marriage was really accidental. She probably would have been frustrated to come all that way expecting to marry someone, only to find the plan foiled.

However, in the end, she would have looked for another husband because the truth was, she hadn't been all that attached to Beckett—clearly, since she'd fallen for another man so rapidly after arriving in Summit County. As a mail-order bride, she'd come west as mostly a stranger to her groom, and at the time, she hadn't been picky and would have taken one man over another as long as they had the qualities she was looking for.

Of course, she felt very differently now that she had Thatcher. She wouldn't be satisfied with just any man. In fact, she couldn't imagine having anyone else but him and never wanted to be with another man ever again.

Including Beckett . . .

They were planning to go over to High Country Ranch to return Weston Oakley's horse today before he left with his little family and returned to Fairplay. Since High Country Ranch was close to the Noble Ranch, Thatcher had suggested they ride out to visit Beckett after returning the horse.

Even though she wanted to put off meeting with Beckett, she knew they no longer had any excuses now that it was the day after Christmas. They needed to let him know about their decision to stay together and then pray he wouldn't protest too strongly or violently.

Last evening, when they'd arrived home from Lee's house and they'd been in the barn tending to Queen together, they'd talked about what to do if Beckett became insistent. Would they need to run off together? And where could they go in December that would be far enough away to be safe?

Not that Beckett had made any physical threats yet. But he'd been clear earlier in the week that he wanted Thatcher to nullify the marriage and that he still wanted to marry her.

She'd suggested they confess the truth to him about falling in love, that they hadn't expected to find love with each other so swiftly and so surely, but it had happened anyway. She hoped Beckett would respect their feelings. At the very least, she hoped he was a decent enough fellow that he wouldn't want to marry her if she was in love with Thatcher. After all, what kind of man would want a woman who loved someone else?

Obviously he'd seemed like a decent fellow from his letters—or what she remembered from them, which wasn't much. And Thatcher claimed Beckett was a good man, having gotten to know him last month while helping the Noble Ranch save their cattle.

Even so, with Beckett holding the loss of his gelding against Thatcher, there was no telling what the ranch foreman might do.

Although Thatcher hadn't said he was nervous about the meeting with Beckett, Amelia could tell he was tense. Thatcher was a healer and not a violent man, but he claimed he wouldn't hesitate to stand his ground if Beckett tried to take Amelia away from him.

But first things first. They were getting the letter to Eileen ready to go in the mail. They were sending it to her New York City address just in case she had been delayed in leaving and still happened to be there.

Amelia could only hope that was the case, but she suspected if that were the reason, the maid would have reached out with another letter by now. After traveling across the country and hearing about train problems, robberies, and even ongoing issues with the natives, Amelia feared that anything could have happened to the young woman.

It was also entirely possible that she could show up today or tomorrow or next week. The chances of that happening were slim, as Thatcher liked to say, because of the difficulty in traversing the mountain passes. But Eileen could have been delayed, similar to what had happened to Amelia.

Regardless, she and Thatcher were doing everything

in their power to fix the mix-up. They'd agreed that only after they'd righted the wrongs would they be able to move forward in their marriage with clear consciences.

She settled a hand on Thatcher's shoulder, amazed that she had the right to touch him like that whenever she wanted and that he welcomed her touch.

Maybe she was simply starved for the connection because she'd never had such a loving and affectionate relationship before. Or maybe she couldn't help but respond to his kindness and tenderness with her, like a newborn creature being nurtured and wanting to show affection in return.

Whatever the case, she wasn't sure she could wait weeks, even months, to resolve the unknown with Eileen before giving in to all that she was feeling for Thatcher, especially because those feelings were growing from foothills into mountains almost overnight.

The mail from the Front Range was sporadic during the winter months, just like the traveling was. But the mail carriers apparently used skis to deliver mail from one town to the next, so it was worth the effort to post the letter.

"So you want to take the letter to town first?" she asked, handing Thatcher the envelope that he'd already addressed.

He folded the sheet. "Yes, and I'm not just saying that to avoid meeting Beckett."

She raised a brow.

"Okay, you're right. I am avoiding the confrontation." He smiled, the smooth motion barreling into her and making her breathless with its charm.

"I suppose there's no harm in putting it off a little longer."

"My thoughts exactly." He slipped the letter into the envelope. "Except that we probably should return Weston's horse first because they'll probably be wanting to leave first thing this morning."

The loss of the horse meant they would be down to one horse for the time being, which would limit her traveling with Thatcher. He'd said she could ride with him on his horse on occasion if the distance wasn't overly far or too strenuous for the horse. Otherwise, she would likely have to stay home more often, at least until Queen was fully healed and able to carry her load. Even though the mare was improving every day, Thatcher said it could still be weeks before Queen would be ready for a rider.

They were bundled up and heading north in no time. The morning air held a nip of cold, but the high-altitude sunshine was warmer than she'd expected, melting the snow and filling the ruts in the road with puddles. The open range spread out in the river valley, making it an ideal place for ranches.

As they rode, Thatcher told her more about the Oakleys and the High Country Ranch, which was closest to his farm and specialized in breeding horses. She'd already learned a little bit about the family, but Thatcher always seemed to know everything about everybody, and she enjoyed hearing his tales.

The wrought-iron Noble Ranch sign and gate were in sight when they glimpsed a lone rider farther down the road. From the hat and the build, it was easy to see the rider was a cowboy and that he was in a hurry.

Thatcher watched the newcomer for a few seconds, then reined in his horse with a frown. "Great. Just great."

Amelia reined in beside him. "What's wrong?"

Thatcher shied back a couple of steps, moving off the road and out of the way. "Looks like we're going to have that meeting with Beckett in a minute."

She peered again at the rider, fresh trepidation swirling in her stomach.

It was easy to tell when Beckett noticed them by the slowing of his mount and the steeling of his shoulders.

She and Thatcher waited silently, the tension increasing with every second. Would Beckett ride past them, or would they have a meeting right here and now on the road?

When he drew up to them, he reined in only a dozen paces away. His brow furrowed in obvious displeasure. It was clear he wasn't passing by without saying or doing something.

She gripped her reins tighter, hoping to keep him

from seeing the tremble in her fingers.

"Beckett." Thatcher spoke the greeting calmly, even though his body was rigid in his saddle. "We were on our way to pay you a visit."

"I was on my way to your place to do the same." Beckett's voice had a distinct Southern drawl that she'd noticed the first time she'd met him.

Amelia wanted to sidle closer to Thatcher, maybe even hide behind him. But she had to stay strong even as the doubts about her worthiness began to creep out of the corners of her mind, where she'd swept them.

She couldn't accept her mother's failures as her own. Instead, she needed to remember she was worthy of love, worthy of having a family, and worthy of having Thatcher.

Beckett tipped up the brim of his Stetson, then met Thatcher's gaze. "I owe you an apology for the things I said about my horse the other day."

The words were so completely unexpected that Amelia could only blink.

Thankfully, as a good conversationalist, Thatcher took the comment in stride. "Thank you, Beckett. I appreciate that."

"No, really. You were only telling me what I already knew. I should have put the horse down earlier. It's just that I'd been hanging on to hope that you could figure out a way to save him."

"And I'm truly sorry there was nothing I could do."

"I know that." Beckett's tone held a note of humility, one that proved he was a good man and that Amelia hadn't been wrong about his character when she'd exchanged letters with him. "I shouldn't have gotten so angry."

"You were grieving—"

"I have no excuse."

"I wish I could have done more."

"You're a good veterinarian, Thatcher. No doubt about it. You did more than most men would last month when you came over and saved the herd."

"I'd do it again in a heartbeat."

Beckett peered off into the distance for a long second, then returned his gaze to them, this time to Amelia. "Ma'am, I'm real sorry for making such a scene about you marrying Thatcher."

She didn't know how to respond, wasn't as smooth as Thatcher. So she just nodded while fingering the beautiful bracelet Thatcher had given her.

"I can see that you thought he was the right fella, and that you made a mistake, plain and simple."

"I did." She swallowed her hesitancy. "I didn't realize it until I found Eileen's letters."

Beckett's gaze bounced between her and Thatcher for a moment. "It's also plain as mud that the two of you already really like each other."

"I love Amelia, Beckett." Thatcher's voice was firm.

"And I love Thatcher." Amelia somehow found her voice, wanting to state her feelings so that Beckett knew she felt the same way as Thatcher and had no intention of giving him up.

"And I'm not planning to nullify the marriage, Beckett." Thatcher sat up in his saddle and squared his shoulders. "I'm planning to keep Amelia forever."

She stiffened, waiting for Beckett's protest.

But Beckett released an almost defeated sigh. "Figured as much."

"We never meant to cause problems," Thatcher said quickly.

"Yep. Well, it put me in a bind. But that isn't your fault."

"What kind of bind?" Thatcher studied Beckett with his usual compassion—just one more thing she loved about Thatcher, that he could so easily forgive.

"Nothin' for you to worry about."

"That's not true." Thatcher patted his coat pocket. "We've got a letter for Eileen right here, hoping to make things right with her and help her out until she can make other arrangements. And we'd like to help you too, if possible."

Beckett gave a half shrug. "That's mighty nice of you, but there's nothin' you can do to help."

"I'll pay for you to put another advertisement into the

marriage catalog."

"I don't have time for that."

"If you write another one up, you'll be able to start writing to someone by spring and maybe send for her over the summer."

Beckett ran a hand down his mouth and over his scruff as though he was debating saying something. Then he met Thatcher's gaze, his blue eyes bleak. "I've got to get married by my thirtieth birthday in May."

"You do?"

"Yep."

Amelia's mind went back to one of the letters she'd received from the men, the one where the fellow had been insistent that she leave right away in the spring and get to Breckenridge no later than May 1. That had to have been Beckett.

But why the need?

Thatcher was watching Beckett as though waiting for more of a revelation as well. "When in May is your birthday?"

"May fifteenth."

Thatcher seemed to be silently calculating the dates.

"It won't work." Beckett's tone held finality. "I already thought through that, and even if I put out a notice today, I wouldn't be able to get a woman here that soon."

"It would be difficult."

Both men fell silent.

"I'm sorry, Beckett," Thatcher finally said.

"Reckon I'll figure something else out."

"And if you don't?" Amelia couldn't hold back the question.

Beckett glanced at her before focusing on his gloved hands, holding the reins of his horse. "It's obvious you're happy with Thatcher, so I don't want you worrying about it."

"But we feel responsible—" she started.

"We want to help," Thatcher said at the same time.

Beckett was quiet for several heartbeats. "Reckon if you hear of a woman looking to get married, you can pass along my name."

Thatcher nodded.

"Would you consider Eileen?" Amelia asked. "She might still be on her way."

Beckett's brows rose with skepticism, but he didn't immediately say no.

"We can add a postscript to the letter to her," Thatcher added, patting his coat pocket again, "and let her know about you."

"We don't know anything about each other."

"She's a very nice woman. But I'll let you read her letters and determine that for yourself."

Amelia had already pulled the letters out from where she'd hidden them. Thankfully, Thatcher had only laughed about the incident.

Beckett pressed his lips together as though he might protest. But then he gave a curt nod. "Maybe."

Amelia allowed herself a full breath for the first time since seeing Beckett riding down the road toward them. Was it really possible he wouldn't oppose her staying with Thatcher?

Thatcher met her gaze, his eyes brimming with hope. *I love you*, he mouthed with a soft smile.

I love you too, she mouthed back, wanting to span the distance between their horses and take his hand in hers. But she held herself back.

Catching sight of their private exchange, Beckett shifted in his saddle and peered at the muddy road.

A part of her felt sorry for him. On the other hand, she was mostly relieved that he was being gracious about letting her out of their bargain.

"Thank you, Beckett," she offered.

"Don't worry about it." He was still focused on the ground. "It appears you're happy with Thatcher, and I know for a fact I wouldn't have been able to make you that happy."

She hadn't expected anyone to make her this happy. But Thatcher did, and she wanted to make him happy in return. "Maybe someday you'll find the right person too, and then you'll be surprised at how much joy you find in the relationship."

He shrugged as if he didn't believe that was possible. "My reason for needing to get married by my birthday is pretty selfish anyway. So if it doesn't happen, it serves me right for trying to use a woman for selfish gain."

"I don't suppose any of us are without some selfish motivation." She only had to think about her situation—the need to escape from her community, the need to get away from Geoff and the danger she'd felt around him, the need for a man to take care of her, the need for a father for her unborn child. All of it had been selfish too, so she couldn't fault Beckett. "We probably wouldn't have signed up for the mail-order service if we didn't have needs."

"Very true," Thatcher responded before Beckett could. "Don't be too hard on yourself, Beckett."

Beckett just gathered up his horse's reins. "I'm heading into town to make sure I clear up the misunderstanding about the gelding. I spouted off at the mouth more than I should have, and I want people to know that none of it was your fault, that it was all mine."

"That's a nice thing to do." Thatcher's horse took a step back, squelching in the mud.

"It's the least I can do to make it up to you." Within seconds, Beckett was riding away, leaving her and Thatcher alone, staring after him in the morning sunshine.

She felt suddenly weak with relief. The situation

could have ended in disaster with someone getting hurt. But thankfully, Beckett had been reasonable and understanding. They'd worked out an arrangement for both Eileen and Beckett—if Eileen was agreeable.

Were she and Thatcher untangled from the mess of their marriage mix-up? She could only hope they were finally free to start a life of their own.

22

"It's not the blackleg," Thatcher said as he finished examining the steer.

He hadn't expected to be called to do any examining—not until Beckett was able to counter the rumors with the truth. But after Weston and his small family had ridden away from High Country Ranch, Maverick Oakley had asked Thatcher to stay and take a look at one of the sick steers.

He'd been more thrilled than he would admit that Maverick had still trusted him enough to ask for his help.

"Appears to be a simple infection. That's all." Thatcher wiped his hand on the towel Amelia was holding for him. She was as attentive and helpful as always.

Outside the isolated stall in a far corner of the barn, Maverick leaned casually against the stall gate. "Relieved to hear it."

The wiry cowboy with his dark hair and dark good looks had apparently charmed many a woman before he'd married his childhood sweetheart. His wife, Hazel, was a talented broodmare manager, and Thatcher had met her on a previous visit out to the ranch. Earlier, she'd stepped out of the mare barn to say goodbye to Weston and Serena and their children, and it was more than clear she was expecting a baby.

She looked to be as far along as Amelia. He hoped the two women would be able to become friends and find encouragement in their motherhood journey together, especially since it looked like he might not be an outcast in the community after all.

It would still take some time before people would start calling on him again for his services, but he was grateful Maverick had given him the chance to prove himself again.

"I can come out this week and vaccinate your steers for blackleg." Thatcher gave the steer a pat on its hindquarter. "Doing so might put your mind at ease."

"Yep, that's what I'm thinking." Maverick had his arms crossed and didn't seem all that worried about the disease. "Heard the vaccine saved Sterling's herd, so I'd be obliged."

"You would be doing me a favor by letting me treat the steers."

"A favor? How so?"

"Nobody trusts me right now." Maybe he shouldn't be so open. But that's just who he was. "So you giving me the job will hopefully help restore confidence in my abilities."

Maverick tipped up the brim of his hat, revealing surprised eyes. "You're not talking about Beckett's whining about his gelding having to be put down, are you?"

"Yes, guess I am." Thatcher started toward the stall exit. "Lost a lot of trust from the incident."

Maverick held his gaze. "Reckon you gained the trust of anyone who knows anything about livestock."

Thatcher halted so quickly that Amelia bumped into him from behind. He reached behind, clasped her arm, and steadied her, but at the same time, he waited for Maverick to explain his statement.

"Took a lot of sensibility," Maverick continued, "to be able to stand your ground on what was best for that horse even if it wasn't the easy decision to make and earned you Beckett's wrath."

"Thank you."

"That's the kind of man I want working around my livestock—one who isn't afraid to stand up for what's right even when it's not popular."

Thatcher's chest welled up with gratitude, so much so that for a moment he couldn't speak.

Amelia's hand squeezed his, as though she understood

what Maverick's words meant to him.

Maverick offered him a grin. "So when can you start on the vaccinations?"

Thatcher made plans to come later in the week, then he helped Amelia onto his horse and climbed up behind her. Maverick offered to let them borrow one of his many horses, but Thatcher explained their situation with Queen and said he didn't mind sharing the mount with Amelia. At his declaration, Maverick grinned again and said he understood all about that.

As Thatcher guided his horse back onto the road and off the Noble Ranch, he allowed himself a breath of relief.

Squeezed into the saddle directly in front of him, Amelia leaned back into his chest. "Have I told you yet today what a good man you are?"

She'd started asking him that whenever he brought up his question—*Have I told you yet today how beautiful you are?*

"You're a good man, Thatcher Hoyt. And the night you walked into the hotel in Breckenridge and decided to marry me was the best day of my life."

"It was the best day of my life too." It was. Maybe messes and mistakes were difficult in the moment, but sometimes Providence had a way of turning those messes and mistakes into miracles. And Amelia was his miracle.

She shifted her head enough that she could brush a kiss to his neck.

As her lips touched him, heat rushed through him, heightening his awareness of every part of his body that had contact with any part of hers. His legs flamed at being tangled against hers. His chest squeezed as her back curved into him. His arms rippled with need as her shoulders and arms brushed his.

There had been a few moments when they'd been close to each other, like Christmas Day, when he'd pulled her down onto his lap. Or one of the first nights, when she'd crawled into bed with him. Of course, they'd shared a couple of amazing kisses.

But they'd done their best to remain respectful of their situation and honor their decision to wait until they made amends with Beckett and Eileen before allowing themselves to express their love more fully.

For some reason, at the moment, Thatcher felt a strange freedom with Amelia that hadn't been there before. Maybe it was because they'd worked things out with Beckett. Maybe it was because they had a plan to help Eileen.

Or maybe their love had blossomed and was now ready for more . . .

Whatever the case, her kiss on his neck liquefied something inside Thatcher, and molten heat began to pump through his veins.

He bent in and placed a kiss against her temple. It ended up being hard and lingering and filled with all the heat coursing inside him. "I love you." His voice was slightly hoarse with need—a need that he'd kept banked but which was now hammering for release.

"And I love you."

It didn't matter that he'd told her how he felt about her a half a dozen times already that day. And it didn't matter that she'd told him the same. He would never tire of saying it or hearing it.

She angled up again and placed another kiss on his neck—this one harder and longer. It contained something that hadn't been there before. This time she pressed in with a demand for more from him.

Was she feeling that blossoming and readiness too?

He didn't want to push her too quickly, but was it time to finally open the door and let their love flow freely without any holding back?

Before he could give himself an excuse to back away, he angled in and captured her lips. They weren't soft and sweet and pliable. Instead, she rose into the kiss with hard, hungry, and demanding lips, and he could do nothing less than respond with the same passion.

The rhythm of their mouths was deep and fast and needy, and it sent his pulse spurting with the same deep and fast and needy tempo.

One of her hands arched around to grasp his neck as though to lock him in place and never let him go. He loved the possessiveness of her hold, and he wrapped one of his arms around her waist and held her possessively too.

Somehow he'd brought the horse to a halt. With the sunshine bathing them in warmth, all he wanted to do was stay there and kiss her until they'd gotten their fill, which he doubted he ever would.

But in the next instant, a gust of north winter wind swirled around them, bringing a cold chill to remind him that they had forever to kiss and didn't need to try to do it all in one day.

As he finished the kiss, he gathered the reins and nudged the horse onward. Then he forced himself to pull back, but only enough that he was still lingering near her cheek and could kiss her dimple.

She dropped her arm from his neck and seemed to reluctantly shift forward in the saddle again.

They rode in silence for several heartbeats, his cheek brushing hers, and his breath mingling with hers.

"Thatcher?" She spoke breathlessly.

"Yes, sweetheart?"

"Could we wait until tomorrow to ride into town to send Eileen's letter instead of going today?"

He couldn't resist kissing her dimple again, the spot so tender and so soft. "Of course, sweetheart. I doubt one day will make much of a difference."

"Good." Her hand shifted to his thigh, her fingers splaying and her thumb rubbing back and forth.

In an instant, her touch ignited him like a torch so that his entire body was on fire.

"Because we have a very busy day ahead of us." She spoke nonchalantly but with a hint of sultriness that only turned up the degree of heat already raging through him.

"Busy?" He could barely get the word out without his voice squeaking.

"Very busy."

He cleared his throat. "Busy how?"

Her lips began to curl up into a smile. "You'll see."

Was it too much to hope that their *busy* day would be filled with lots of kissing? "Can you give me a hint?"

"I already did. But just in case it wasn't clear before . . ." She twisted and fused her lips with his again, just as hard and needy as the last kiss—maybe even more so. It was over before he could respond, and she was settling back against him, this time with a beautiful smile.

He let his smile loose too. "I think I'm going to enjoy our day very much."

"I think I will too."

He wrapped her up closer. "I'm going to enjoy *every* day with you, Amelia. From now until forever." And he knew that no matter where he was or what he was doing, as long as he had her, he would be a happy man.

23

"Thata girl," Amelia, at the center of the corral, crooned to Queen as the horse trotted in a circle. "You're looking beautiful and strong."

The early March day held a hint of spring. The sunshine was warm on Amelia's head and on her face. Though the heaviest snowfalls and cold of the high-country winter had passed according to Thatcher, he insisted they could still have plenty more snow and cold before summer came.

Over the past weeks, Queen had healed well. Although she wasn't ready yet to have a rider, she was able to move again. Thatcher predicted she would probably be ready to bear weight in about a month. Although Amelia had enjoyed riding with Thatcher on his horse, the saddle had quickly grown too small as the baby grew. Thatcher had finally agreed to borrow one of Maverick Oakley's horses, but only as payment for helping to vaccinate High

Country Ranch's cattle from blackleg.

Amelia rested a hand on her abdomen, which was well-rounded and getting even bigger with every passing day. Thatcher had started collecting baby equipment and furniture, always coming back from town with one item or another, possibly more excited about the baby than even she was.

As Rusty stood and began to wag his tail and limp down the lane, she lifted a hand to her eyes to shield them, squinting in the direction of town. Sure enough, a horse and rider were visible through the trees. Thatcher was home.

Her heart thudded with an extra beat at the prospect of being in his arms in just moments. Being against him and in his arms was her favorite spot to be, and she spent as much time as possible there.

She smiled and ducked her head, almost embarrassed at how much time they spent in each other's arms. She knew their days and nights would soon be filled with taking care of the baby and eventually more children. But for now, she was enjoying these few months of having Thatcher to herself. And he made it obvious every day that he was enjoying it too.

"That's a good effort today, Your Majesty." Amelia stepped up to Queen and took her lead line. "Time for a rest."

Amelia brushed a hand down the horse's glossy black

flank, her bracelet jangling with a new little button of a baby chick because she'd single-handedly saved an entire batch of abandoned chicks from dying by tending to them for days.

Once her baby was born, she knew she wouldn't be able to go with Thatcher quite as often. He'd indicated his mother had often brought him and his siblings along with her when she'd still been assisting her father and that they'd loved going. Amelia hoped she could figure out a way to do that too.

As it was, she was slowing down—or at least trying to—so that she didn't cause the baby any problems. She hated being away from Thatcher even for a few hours, but the time apart always made their reunions sweet.

As the pounding of Thatcher's horse's hooves drew nearer, she crossed to the corral gate and exited just as he turned the bend around the cabin and came into full view. The sight of him, as always, sent a flush of rapid desire through her. She loved everything about him from his sturdy frame to his bulky shoulders to his thick legs. He was built of solid split rails, strong and secure.

He tipped up his hat, revealing his wide, boyish face with all its charm. His eyes were alight and his smile already in place.

She lifted a hand in greeting and smiled back, the happiness of seeing him swelling in her chest and making her wonder how she'd ever gotten along without him.

The truth was, she hadn't. He'd been the one to show her she had worth and how to really live, and she was grateful every day for the mail-order-bride mix-up that had brought them together.

In the next moment, he was reining in and dismounting. She was right there waiting, and he stepped in and wrapped her up in his arms.

"I missed you," he whispered as he pressed a kiss against her head.

She loved that he was so expressive and never shy about telling her how he felt. And it amazed her that he always felt so strongly about her, missing her and loving her and appreciating her.

She nestled in against him and breathed out a contented sigh. Only one thing would make her more content, and that was kissing him. She pushed back enough from him that she could rise up on her toes and capture his mouth in a hungry kiss.

He kissed her back hungrily for only a moment before pulling away.

She started to protest, wrapping her arms around his neck and intending to drag him back down.

But he tugged something out of his pocket. "I got a letter from Eileen."

Amelia froze. It had been over two months since they'd sent the letter to Eileen about their marriage mix-up. A part of Amelia had just wanted to forget all about

Eileen and hope they never heard back from her. Another part of her wanted Eileen to come and agree to marry Beckett, who was still counting on that possibility before his thirtieth birthday.

Thatcher released her and then held up the envelope.

"What does it say?" Amelia asked.

"I haven't opened it yet. I was waiting to read it with you." His eyes held a gravity now that seemed to match the gravity that had fallen over Amelia.

She nodded and then watched wordlessly as Thatcher opened the envelope, took out a sheet, and unfolded it.

"'Dear Thatcher,'" he started, "'thank you for your letter informing me of how your circumstances have changed. I would have done the same, but I became very ill for many weeks and was unable to write to you regarding my delay. I was nearly on my deathbed at one point and feared I would not live, much less marry. I am recovering now finally, but I am not strong enough, and may never again be, to travel across the country. So I do release you from any obligation to me. It would appear the mail-order-bride mix-up was for the best. I wish you all the best in your marriage. Sincerely, Eileen. P.S. I do thank you for the suggestion of another man there who is willing to wed me, but I regret that I cannot take up the offer.'"

When Thatcher finished reading it, he looked at Amelia, his eyes wide with wonder.

A sense of relief washed through Amelia. "I'm sorry for Eileen's illness, but I cannot deny that I'm glad she's not still expecting to get married to you."

"I feel the same way." Thatcher scanned the letter again, silently rereading it. "The only trouble is that I was hoping she'd be willing to marry Beckett."

Before mailing their original letter to Eileen, Amelia and Thatcher had added a postscript suggesting the possibility of marrying another man in the area, one who would be agreeable to the arrangement. After meeting Beckett on the road that day, they'd felt it was only right to do so.

"Beckett will be disappointed." Thatcher peered north in the direction of the Noble Ranch.

"Yes, but he also understood it was only a possibility and not a certainty."

They'd encountered Beckett a few times over the past couple of months, and he'd been gracious to them, had even apologized to Thatcher again. True to his word, Beckett had helped repair Thatcher's reputation, letting everyone know that he'd been the one in the wrong about his gelding and not Thatcher. Of course, people had continued to call on Thatcher for his services, many, like Maverick, respecting Thatcher even more as a result of the incident.

Whatever the case, Beckett would be in a bind if he didn't find a wife soon. Amelia didn't know what he would do to find a woman by May, but she would pray that somehow things would work out for him—not only in finding a wife but also in falling in love.

Now that she'd fallen in love, she'd seen firsthand the blessings, and she was more than desirous that others get their chance at love too.

Thatcher began to fold the letter. "Let's pray for Providence to provide a miracle for Beckett the same way He did for me."

Amelia smiled up at him. "So I'm your miracle, am I?"

"Yes, you are." He tucked the letter in his duster pocket and then reached for her.

She went to him willingly—*more* than willingly. As he wrapped her up against him, she wound her arms around his neck, eager for his touch and his closeness. "I love you."

"I love you too, sweetheart, more than you could ever know." His blue eyes reflected the cloudless sky and contained an endless love.

She tipped up the brim of his cowboy hat and lifted on her toes so that her lips were almost touching his. "You were and always will be my favorite cowboy."

Then she pressed her lips to his and showed him just how much she favored him over everyone and everything.

Author's Note

Hi, dear readers!

Thank you for joining me on another adventure in Colorado's beautiful high country. I hope you enjoyed getting to see Thatcher and Amelia's very mixed-up mail-order-bride situation work out for them. It sure was a fun story to write, getting them to fall in love and then find out they were each meant for someone else!

You're probably wondering what happens to Beckett now that Eileen is no longer coming! Well, saddle up for another adventure, this one for Beckett to find his true love. What is Beckett hiding, and will he be able to find true love by his thirtieth birthday? Poor Beckett still has a lot to learn about love and sacrifice, but don't worry, he'll get his happily ever after too!

In the meantime, if you missed Weston and Serena's love story, then you really should go pick up a copy today! *Claiming the Cowgirl* is a short novel that brings this couple together in a marriage of convenience. With both of them haunted by their pasts, can they find a way to heal and move into a love relationship before it's too late? Obviously, you already know they do find a way to be together. But now you get to find out how! To give you a taste of their story, I've included chapter one.

As always, I love hearing from YOU! If you haven't yet joined my Facebook Reader Room, what are you waiting for!? It's a great place to keep up-to-date on all my book releases and book news, as well as a fun place to connect with other readers and me.

Farewell, but not for long!

Other books in the Noble Ranch series as of 2025 (with plenty more to come!):

The Forever Cowboy

After running away from her wedding and hiding for months, Violet Berkley is back home in the high country of Colorado. Her father's gambling debt has caught up to him, and he wants Violet and her sister to help him pay it off by working as dancing girls in a saloon. Rather than face such degradation, Violet seeks out the one man she hopes might be willing to help her.

READ ON FOR AN EXCERPT OF
CLAIMING THE COWGIRL
(Weston and Serena's story)

COLORADO
COWGIRLS
5
CLAIMING
THE COWGIRL
JODY HEDLUND

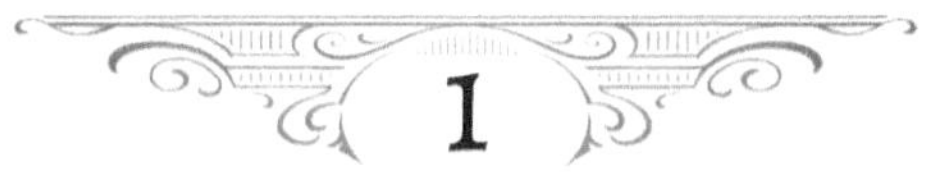

1

She had to stop procrastinating and force herself to pick a new husband.

Serena Taylor tucked her list of potential husbands into the pocket of her day dress. She'd crossed out all but four of the men who lived in the Fairplay area. But maybe just four was narrowing her choice too much?

The bitter December wind coming off the mountains swirled around her, and she hugged Tate closer to protect his plump cheeks from the chill. Burrowing against her chest, he sucked his thumb, content to ride on her hip for as long as she could carry him—which were shorter periods now that he was two and growing bigger every day.

"Only one more visit," she whispered against his

forehead before brushing a kiss to his silky light brown hair that was a shade fairer than hers. "Then we'll head home."

Home? She hadn't had a home since running away two months ago from Stony Creek Ranch near Pueblo. Even then, the large spread hadn't felt like home in the few years she'd lived there with Palmer and his parents. It had felt even less so after her husband's death this past summer. In fact, life there had become oppressive—so much so that she'd decided to move back to Oklahoma and live with her family.

She hadn't anticipated that her father-in-law would not only agree that she move away but require her to relinquish her rights to Tate and let him raise her child. When she'd protested, Mr. Halifax's solicitor had presented her with a legal document claiming that a single woman was an unfit mother, mentally unstable, financially irresponsible, and unable to raise a child.

Mr. Halifax was a hard man who always got what he wanted one way or another. So, with only as much of her belongings as would fit into a carpetbag, Serena had ridden away in the middle of the night, afraid that if she stayed even one more day, she'd never see Tate again.

She hadn't known where to go, just that she couldn't return to Oklahoma since it would be the first place Mr. Halifax would look for her. So, she'd traveled to the South Park area until she'd reached Fairplay, and her money had run out.

At least the Courtney Boardinghouse had been a safe haven for the past weeks she'd lived there, working to earn her room and board.

But as she'd learned early in life, all good things had to come to an end eventually. And she couldn't stay at the boardinghouse indefinitely. Not if she hoped to keep Tate. No, she had to stop putting off the one thing that could alleviate all her worries about losing him to Palmer's parents. She had to get remarried. And the sooner, the better.

Serena straightened her petite frame and squared her shoulders, then started down the boardwalk of Fairplay's business district, heading to her final destination and the fourth candidate on her list—Mr. Dankworth, the owner of the mercantile at the end of Main Street. He was a widower with several small children and seemed like a good father.

A good father. That was her number one qualification for a husband. She didn't care how he treated her. As long as he cared about Tate, that's all that mattered.

Well, of course, she also wanted him to be a God-fearing, upright, and law-abiding man. He had to be able to provide financially for her and Tate so that Mr. Halifax would have no reason to question whether Tate's every need was being met.

Her father-in-law was powerful and wealthy, with

enough connections that he would learn of her whereabouts eventually—if he hadn't already. And although the mountain passes were now covered in snow and made traveling difficult, Mr. Halifax wouldn't let that stop him from tracking her to the high country.

Hopefully, once she was legally remarried, her father-in-law's accusations would no longer have any merit. At least then her new husband could help her keep custody of Tate.

In the late afternoon, Fairplay's streets weren't yet busy with miners and mill employees who would soon finish work and head to their boardinghouses and the saloons. Even so, the rattle of passing wagons and the clatter of horses mingled with the calls and greetings of the townspeople—mostly men—milling about.

At least she hadn't faced a shortage of marriageable options. In this mountainous area miles from the big cities, men outnumbered women by far. Although Fairplay was a thriving town and had some families, as a single, widowed woman she'd attracted plenty of male attention.

Of course, she needed the right man and couldn't just settle for anyone, which was why she'd been so carefully whittling her list down over recent weeks. The men on her list obviously hadn't realized the so-called chance encounters were interviews, but with each trip into town, she'd purposefully orchestrated time with the candidates so she could get to know them better and see how they interacted with Tate.

Now, with only four remaining on the list, she'd done the same today. She'd coordinated the meetings with each and had only Mr. Dankworth left.

When she finished visiting him, would she finally be able to make her choice?

With her boots tapping firmly against the wooden plank boardwalk, she neared the two-story false storefront with the name *Dankworth's* painted in bold letters above the wooden awning.

Her arms had begun to ache from carrying Tate, but once she reached the interior, she'd set him down as she browsed the wares she couldn't afford and wouldn't be purchasing. Hopefully, Mr. Dankworth would come out from behind his counter and talk to her as he had the past several times she'd stopped in. His oldest daughter, who appeared to be about eight years old, took care of her siblings and had been kind to Tate. Would Mr. Dankworth's children welcome a new brother into their family?

At the door, she paused and straightened her hat—a Gainsborough with round crown and a brim turned up on one side. Navy blue and trimmed with flowers, it was starting to grow shabby, just like the rest of the few garments she'd brought along.

Lifting her chin in resolve, she opened the door to the

scent of leather and tobacco as well as the welcoming warmth emanating from the potbellied stove at the center of the store, a coal bin and spittoon beside it.

Floor-to-ceiling shelves lined most walls and were crammed with every conceivable item—canned foods, spices, crockery, fabric, sewing notions, and medicines. The countertops ran the length of one side, and they were piled with ready-made clothing, blankets, hats, and more. Horse whips and farming tools hung from the ceiling.

Several other customers were in the store: an older man near the back examining harnesses, a fellow sitting in a chair near the stove and reading a newspaper, and another man at the counter—a tall, dark-haired man she immediately recognized.

Weston Oakley. He had lean facial features with a squared jawline, a prominent chin with a noticeable cleft, and a nose with a slight dorsal bump. His coat stretched tightly across his broad shoulders and thickly-muscled arms. And his torso and legs radiated equal strength, although his wool trousers hung more loosely and were tucked into worn leather boots.

"My family doesn't think I'm capable of getting married," Weston was saying. "And if I don't round up a wife by Christmas, they'll never leave me alone."

The very handsome Weston Oakley had recently belonged to Felicity Courtney. Perhaps *belonged* wasn't the right word, but the two had been nearly engaged. The rumor was that Weston had even built a house for her.

However, Felicity had broken Weston's heart when she'd married someone else and moved away.

Serena liked Felicity. After all, Felicity had been the one running the boardinghouse and had taken her in during her time of need.

But Serena wished Felicity hadn't hurt Weston so terribly. She hadn't been fair to the kind, hard-working man. Although Serena had contemplated making him number five on her list of potential husbands, she'd witnessed firsthand the heartache he'd experienced from Felicity's rejection, and she'd seen the misery in his expression ever since.

She'd concluded that he wasn't ready to form another relationship so soon after losing Felicity. But what if she was wrong?

As the door closed behind her and she stepped farther into the store, every eye shifted her way, including Mr. Dankworth's and Weston's.

"Good afternoon, Mrs. Taylor." Mr. Dankworth stood suddenly straighter, adjusting his bow tie and collar before slicking back his thinning brown hair. On the shorter side of average, Mr. Dankworth wore an apron over his suit, which seemed overly large on his trim frame.

"Ma'am." Though Weston nodded at her politely, his blue-black eyes flitted over her and dismissed her all in one motion—just as usual.

Also just as usual, his gaze came to rest on Tate.

The boy lifted his head from her shoulder and slid his thumb out of his mouth. Now he was staring at Weston with his wide green eyes—the color another trait she and Tate shared.

"Hey there, little fella." Weston offered Tate a tender smile.

"Ball?" Tate asked timidly.

Serena lowered Tate to the ground. He promptly latched on to her skirt, clinging to her as he always did whenever they were around other people. She had to stifle the urge to flex her arms and stretch the ache out of her back.

"Sorry." Weston stuffed his hands in his pockets. "I don't have a ball today."

The last time she and Tate had encountered Weston was several days ago at church. When Tate had gotten restless during the service, Weston, from the pew behind them, had handed Tate a marble to play with.

She'd been grateful for Weston's consideration, especially when he'd insisted afterward that Tate could keep the marble, since he'd apparently picked it up off the street and had no use for it.

Weston pulled a hand out of his pocket and held out a stick of light-pink candy. "I've got this candy . . . if your ma says it's okay for you to eat."

At the sight of the offering, Tate's beautiful eyes

rounded even more. He shifted his questioning gaze up to her. "Candy, Mama?"

How could she say no when his face was filled with such innocence and sweetness? He'd had so few pleasures during his short life—had more frightening experiences than anything. Besides, with the little she earned working at the boardinghouse, she didn't have much to spare for simple gifts.

She brushed his hair out of his eyes. "Alright."

Tate released his grip on her skirt and took a tentative step toward Weston. Then, in a burst, he raced the last of the distance. As he took the stick, Weston ruffled Tate's hair.

"What do you say to the nice man?" Serena prompted.

Tate was already running back to her side, his eyes containing an equal measure of both fright and excitement. As he latched on to her skirt again, she tucked a finger under his chin and leveled stern eyes upon him. "Tell Mr. Oakley *thank you.*"

"Thank you." Tate's voice was so soft she doubted anyone heard him.

But Weston nodded, then gathered up a parcel from the counter, tipped the brim of his black Stetson toward Mr. Dankworth, and crossed to the door, his boots clunking against the wooden floorboards. As he passed by, he ruffled Tate's hair again. "Enjoy the candy, little fella."

Then, with a polite touch of the brim of his hat in farewell to her, he exited the mercantile.

She couldn't keep from watching him through the glass panes on the front door as he crossed the street and seemed to head toward the bank. His stride was long and determined, and he carried himself with strength and purpose, as though the whole world yet needed his conquering.

After his declaration to Mr. Dankworth about needing a wife by Christmas, did she dare turn him into her fifth matrimonial candidate?

He always interacted so thoughtfully with Tate, and Tate seemed to be drawn to him the most, even aside from the gifts of the marble and candy.

Yes, Weston Oakley would most definitely qualify to be on her list. The question was, would he consider marrying her after his recent heartache? He hardly seemed to realize she existed—probably wouldn't regard her at all if not for Tate.

"What can I do for you today, Mrs. Taylor?" Still behind the counter, Mr. Dankworth had donned a wide and welcoming smile, appreciation lighting up his face as it normally did whenever he looked at her.

Like the other three candidates, he was always eager for her visits, going out of his way to talk with her and pay her compliments. He hadn't yet proposed as the others had, but she predicted it wouldn't be long before he did.

She could have her choice of the four.

But shouldn't she at least test Weston and determine if he was a possibility too?

For a long moment her mind spun, doing what it did so well—scheming and plotting to make circumstances work to her advantage. As an idea began to evolve, she nodded at Mr. Dankworth and turned to the door. "I guess I won't be needing anything today after all. But I do thank you for the offer."

With Tate clinging to her skirt and sucking on his candy, she exited the mercantile. She had to hurry if she had any hope of facilitating a *chance* meeting with Weston before darkness fell.

Hopefully, this time he would take more notice of her and perhaps even consider her a prospect for the wife he needed by Christmas.

Jody Hedlund is the bestselling author of more than sixty novels and is the winner of numerous awards. Jody lives in Michigan with her husband, busy family, and five spoiled cats. She writes sweet historical romances with plenty of sizzle.

A complete list of my novels can be found at jody hedlund.com.

Would you like to know when my next book is available? You can sign up for my newsletter, become my friend on Goodreads, like me on Facebook, or follow me on Instagram.

Newsletter: jodyhedlund.com
Facebook: AuthorJodyHedlund
Instagram: @JodyHedlund